THE BANDITS OF WHISKEY CITY
(Book 2 of the Whiskey City Series)
Robin Gibson

The misadventures of young sheriff Teddy Cooper continue in this second book of **The Whiskey City Series** as Teddy and four men head out of Whiskey City to buy cattle. An ambush by an unlikely band of varmints leave the five men stranded in the plains with nothing but their underwear and wounded pride.

The journey to track down the bandits takes a very ugly turn as the motley gang from Whiskey City become suspects in a bank robbery. Determined to prove their innocence, Teddy and his compadres suddenly find themselves pitted against the notorious Riley Hunt and his men. Will the men from Whiskey City survive this action-packed, bullet-dodging adventure to resume the chase for the bandits?

Cover illustration by Ken Spencer
Cover design by Gordon Haber

THE BANDITS OF WHISKEY CITY

Book Two in The Whiskey City Series

•

ROBIN GIBSON

AVALON BOOKS
THOMAS BOUREGY AND COMPANY, INC.
401 LAFAYETTE STREET
NEW YORK, NEW YORK 10003

Library of Congress Catalog Card Number: 94-096847
ISBN 0-8034-9112-3

PRINTED IN THE UNITED STATES OF AMERICA
ON ACID-FREE PAPER
BY HADDON CRAFTSMEN, SCRANTON, PENNSYLVANIA

To my sister, Nancy

Chapter One

Being robbed ain't no picnic, and we was durned sure robbed. They took everything but the shirts on our backs. Looking back on it, I reckon we shoulda cut our losses, licked our wounds and scooted back home with our tails tucked. It would have saved everybody a wagonload of grief. But we weren't that smart. To this day, I blame them kids, 'cause it all started with them.

Now, I've heard folks say that kids are a blessing. Thinking on it, I reckon the feller who said that was either plumb loco or never met up with any of the little devils . . . certainly not the pack of brats we stumbled upon.

Now, I'll admit that my own experience with youngsters is a mite on the skimpy side, but the few

I have run across gave me a first-rate education on the subject.

We first ran into the little devils five days' ride from home. There was six of us in our party, bound for Arizona to pick up a herd of cattle.

We were a quarter of a mile away when we first spotted them. From a distance, we couldn't tell they were just kids. If we coulda just seen that, we likely woulda turned tail and run. But not us, no, sir, we rode right up to them like a pack of fools.

Oh, we loosened up our guns and fanned out a bit, but we were expecting normal trouble. You know, like outlaws and killers. Really, I would have preferred killers. A whole pack of the West's most bloodthirsty killers couldn't have caused half the trouble them danged kids did.

Them kids, there was three of them, two girls and a boy, perched on a big rock, holding a big carpetbag apiece. They never even turned a hair as we rode up. They just looked up at us innocently with big brown eyes. I reckon that innocent look was what threw us off our guard.

"What are you kids doing out here by yourselves?" I asked, looking around for their folks and having a hard time actually believing they were alone. I mean, the oldest girl was only fourteen, maybe fifteen, and that boy, he couldn't be more than twelve.

"Who are you?" the boy asked.

"My name is Teddy Cooper. I'm the sheriff over at Whiskey City," I answered. "Now, who are you kids and what are you doing way out here?"

"Who are they?" that scrawny boy asked, jabbing a finger at my friends.

"They're friends of mine. Now, who are you?"

"Are they deputies?"

"No, they're just friends."

"Are you chasing outlaws?"

"No," I answered, my voice tight as I fought my temper. "Why don't you let your sisters talk for a spell. They are your sisters?"

The boy looked at me crookedly, a look of doubt on his face. "Sure they are. Are you sure you are a sheriff?"

"Of course, I'm a sheriff," I said, pointing to the badge on my chest. "See my badge."

"Well, you sure don't act smart enough to be a sheriff."

Why, that little . . . I took a step forward, ready to turn that little whippersnapper over my knee and impress some manners on his backside.

"Whoa, boy," Bobby Stamper said, laughing as he grabbed my arm and hauled me back. "Boy, he's sure got you figured out," Stamper said, still chuckling. Bobby was my partner and soon to be my brother-in-law, but we didn't always see eye to eye. Bobby had a devil-may-care attitude about most things, and I'm a cautious sort of man.

"Aw, shut up," I grumbled. I twisted away from Stamper and grabbed that little whipper by the shoulders. "Listen, you little brat, I want some answers. How come you are out here all by yourself?"

"I ain't by myself. My sisters are with me."

"I can see that! What I want to know is where are your folks?" I asked, balling up my fists and fighting my temper.

"I ain't supposed to tell," The brat screamed, slobbering in my face. Then, before I knew it, he hauled off and kicked me in the shins.

Bellering, I let go of the kid, grabbing my smarting leg. Still rubbing my leg, I glared at that kid. Then I growled and started to grab him again. This time I'd show that brat some manners, even if I had to pound them in. Well, before I could grab him, I found myself staring dead ahead at the muzzle of an old pistol.

"You just get away from me and my sisters, mister," the boy said, his voice even.

My so-called fine friends looked at each other, grinning from ear to ear. They could afford to grin; they didn't have that old hogleg shoved in their snoots. Me, I couldn't even get a smile started.

Still smiling tolerantly, Preacher Tom Briscoe stepped up to the youngsters. Kneeling down, Tom took off his hat, his wild, gray hair springing away from his head in every direction. "You're a little green behind the ears to be packing a shootin' iron," Preacher Tom said, holding out his hand. "Now, why don't you pass that thing over to me, and we'll see what we can do to help you and your sisters out.''

Now for a preacher man, ol' Tom was a rough sort of a gent, and wild looking as a hurricane. He was used to dealing with hard cases, but he wasn't nowhere near ready for Junior. That boy turned that pistol on Preacher Tom. ''I done told you, we don't need your help. My paw is coming to get us.''

''Who's your pa?'' I asked.

The boy looked up at me, a look of pride shining in his dirty face. ''Riley Hunt.''

''Where is your pa, now?'' Preacher Tom asked, leaning away from the pistol.

''Teddy,'' I heard Bobby Stamper call, but I paid no mind to him. I was too busy fuming and plotting what I was going to do to that little brat once I got that gun away from him. ''Teddy,'' Bobby yelled, grabbing me and nearly jerking me outta my boots.

''What?'' I asked, keeping my eye on that kid.

''You ever hear of Riley Hunt?'' Bobby asked, dragging me away.

''No, should I have?''

''Being a lawman, I figured you might have heard of him. There's enough Wanted posters out on him to paper an outhouse,'' Bobby answered simply.

''He's an outlaw, then?''

Stamper laughed, pounding me on the back. ''An outlaw? He's worse than that. If they were going to make a list of the meanest men in the world, Riley

Hunt would take the top five or six spots all by hisself.''

''You think those are his kids?'' I asked, scratching my head.

Stamper shrugged. ''I heard Riley had a wife back in Kansas. I never heard of any kids. But who knows?''

''Well, if you ask me, that sawed-off little prairie pup is just the kind of kid a hired killer would have,'' I said, staring at the kids and cursing under my breath as Junior stuck his tongue out at me.

''We'll have to take them with us,'' Bobby decided.

''Aw, do we have to?'' I said and groaned. I could only dream how much trouble them two girls would be, but I could just look at that little brat and tell he would be a handful. I reckon Bobby was right; we had to take them along. I didn't like it much, though.

The flat bark of a pistol jerked me rudely out of my thoughts and made me jump. In a heartbeat, I hauled out my pistol, searching around for the danger.

Preacher Tom stood frozen, a small wisp of dirt rising from the ground between his feet. Now, I don't rightly know if he was scared or just swallered his wad of tobacco, but that preacher man looked a mite green.

While we stood there, our mouths hanging open, that boy cocked his pistol, and them girls whipped out hoglegs from their carpetbags. ''Drop all your guns, or I'll shoot this crusty old geezer,'' the boy threatened.

Even the green color drained from ol' Tom's face and he turned pale as death. "Do what he says," Preacher Tom whispered, his eyes glued to the spot between his legs where the bullet had struck.

"Yeah, drop 'em," the younger girl said, and I almost laughed. Why she couldn't have been more than nine or ten and cute as a button, with a pile of blonde curly hair. She wasn't very big either, I could hardly see her behind that big dragoon colt she pointed at me.

I had my gun out, but I couldn't shoot these little tykes. What I could do was jerk them out of their socks and fan their backsides. With that very thought in mind, I tossed down my gun and took a step forward. The sound of the hammer coming back on that big Colt stopped me dead in my tracks.

It didn't stop Karl Wiesmulluer. That old man had ruled the roost too long. He expected folks to snap to when he barked. He was forever throwing his weight around and jumping headfirst into all kinds of grief. Well, it didn't work this time. When he up and made a grab for that little girl, he grabbed onto trouble with both hands. Now, I ain't rightly sure she meant to shoot, but that big hogleg went off. The bullet whipped Wiesmulluer's hat off his head and flung it ten yards away. His gumption and the color from his face disappeared in the same instant.

To make a long story short, we found ourselves facedown in the grass, cinched up like a bucking saddle.

Them danged kids took everything we had, even our boots and pants. Well, they did leave us our shirts and long johns. That was just because with our hands tied, they couldn't get them off. While we growled and cussed, they gathered our horses and rode off. I'll say one thing for them kids, they knew how to tie a knot. It was night 'fore we got loose.

Morning came, and we started tracking them kids, but we didn't get an early start. Before we could start, we had to do a lot of stomping and cussing. With that wore out of our systems, we set out, five grim-jawed men with murder in our eyes.

A mile of walking didn't improve any of our tempers, but at least them kids were leaving a trail a blind man could follow. Then the tracks turned off the trail, heading up into the hills.

We stopped, milling around in circles and picking stickers out of our feet. Preacher Tom looked down the trail, scratching his beard like a man pulling weeds. "What do we do now?" he asked.

"It's not far into Miles City. We could run into town and get an outfit," Louis Claude suggested as he rubbed his feet. Claude was a farmer by nature and still wasn't sold on the idea of going into the cattle business. He and Wiesmulluer had never gotten along until just recently, and every time one of them spoke I expected them to break out into an argument.

"No way!" Wiesmulluer shouted, shaking his head. "If we leave the trail now, we might never find them kids. I say, we keep after the little buggers till we run them into the ground. I've got a willow switch and I'm just aching to use it."

"You want to go traipsing around barefoot and in our long johns?" Preacher Tom asked. "Do you think we could ever catch them?"

"I'll catch them if it's the last thing I ever do!" Wiesmulluer thundered, smacking his fist into his palm.

To tell the truth, I kinda liked Mr. Claude's idea, but I knew from experience, how mule-stubborn Wiesmulluer could be. "Maybe we should run on into Miles City," I pleaded, looking to the others for support. "We could get an outfit and come right back."

"How are we supposed to put an outfit together? We don't have any money," Wiesmulluer argued.

"There's a bank in Miles City," Bobby Stamper suggested.

Necks popped as we all jerked around to stare at Bobby. "You're married to my daughter now. You're not going back to robbing banks!" Wiesmulluer growled, thumping Bobby in the chest with a bony finger.

Bobby smiled, plastering an innocent look on his face as he spread his hands in front of him. "Who said anything about robbing the joint? What I meant was, we could ask them for a loan.''

``Aw, come on, Bobby. Look at us,'' I said and snorted. ``You think if we walk into a bank like this, they are going to give us money?''

``Louey and Karl are respected businessmen,'' Bobby said, gesturing to Wiesmulluer and Claude. ``Karl has a big ranch and Louey has a nice little farm. Their credit ought to be good.''

``We're a long way from home, Bobby,'' Mr. Claude said, shaking his head and patting Bobby on the back. ``We don't know anyone in Miles City. No, I'm afraid we need to come up with a new plan.''

``Why don't we split up,'' I suggested. ``Part of us could stay on the trail while the rest of us run into town.''

``Good idea,'' Wiesmulluer barked. ``Me and Teddy will follow them runts while the rest of you get us an outfit.''

What! I whipped my head around, staring at that old man. This wasn't at all what I had in mind. I figured to be in the group going to town. I sure didn't want to be stuck out on the trail with Wiesmulluer.

``We'll mark the trail. You ought to be able to catch right up.'' Having spoke his piece, Wiesmulluer squared his shoulders and went to tracking. ``Let's go, Teddy,'' he barked, without even looking back.

For a minute, I didn't move, looking back at the others for help. Nobody seemed inclined to help me out; they just stared at the ground. Cursing my luck, I branded the whole bunch of them with a mean look, then loped after Wiesmulluer.

Now, being barefoot didn't stop him from setting a tough pace. I gritted my teeth, determined not to let an old man outdo me, but it wasn't easy. I don't know what the soles of that old man's feet were made of, but it had to be tough stuff. While I picked my way like a dainty lady, he stomped along grinding his teeth, paying no mind to the stickers and sharp rocks on the trail.

We spent the rest of the morning marching after them kids, coming up to a shabby cabin just shy of noon. The tracks led past the place, swinging a wide circle around the cabin, but we didn't stay with the trail.

"Let's go down," Wiesmulluer said with a grunt, swinging his arm at the cabin. "Maybe we can borrow some clothes and a couple of horses."

"Do we have to?" I said and groaned, almost begging. "If we keep after them kids, we'll catch them pretty soon."

"Catch them?" Wiesmulluer snorted. "We're losing ground fast. At this rate, we'll never catch them."

He was right, but I didn't like it. I could see the woman's clothes hanging on the line behind the cabin. I figured there must be womenfolk down there and didn't want to go prancing down there in my drawers.

Wiesmulluer had no such worries. He grabbed me by the arm and plowed down the rocky slope with me bouncing along behind like a kite tail. He rambled right up to the door like he owned the place. He peeked in the window, then hammered on the door with his fist.

Standing outside that cabin, I felt a bad feeling rushing over me. Looking around, I saw nothing out of the ordinary, but I couldn't shake a feeling of doom.

As the door latch rattled, I shrank back, expecting disaster. What opened the door wasn't a disaster. Oh no, it was far worse. It was a woman. And not your ordinary woman neither. She was an ox of a woman, standing nearly as tall as me, with meat on her frame to match. I swear, this woman was fit to rassle bears. Her rough, red face lit up as she saw us, or rather as she saw Wiesmulluer. She didn't hardly spare me a glance, which she ogled over Wiesmulluer like he'd been dipped in honey.

"My, my, what have we here?" she exclaimed, touching Wiesmulluer's sleeve. "I must say, you boys sure travel light," she added, rubbing his arm as she looked him up and down.

"We were robbed on the trail," Wiesmulluer mumbled, his ears turning red as rhubarb pie.

She lifted her hand and stroked Wiesmulluer's cheek. "You poor dears, it must have been awful for you. Set upon by ruffians. Did they hurt you?"

By now, even the roots of Wiesmulluer's white hair glowed bright crimson. He squirmed, looking like a fishing worm dangling on the line. He looked at me for support, but I turned away, trying not to laugh. "No, they just took everything we owned," he stammered, shifting his feet.

Wiesmulluer pulled himself up to his full height, throwing back his shoulders. He cleared his throat, taking a deep breath. "We were wondering, ma'am, if we could borrow some supplies, and maybe a couple of mounts?"

She placed her hand on his chest, purring as she nuzzled against him. "Well, of course you can, sugar," she murmured, then exclaimed. "Dear me, what am I thinking of? You must be starved. Do come in. I'll fix you a quick bite.

"That's most kind, ma'am, but we really don't have the time. You see, we're on the trail of them hooligans right now."

That woman, she didn't pay the slightest bit of attention to what Wiesmulluer said. She just pulled him inside. I tagged along behind, the mention of food catching my interest.

"Sit down at the table," she instructed, finally letting go of Wiesmulluer's arm. She crossed to the stove and dished us up a couple bowls of stew from the big pot on the stove. She placed the bowls in front of us, along with a loaf of bread. "Eat this. I'll go find you some duds."

I didn't need no second invitation. I tore into that stew like a house afire. I was nearly finished with my bowl when the woman returned with two bundles of clothes.

"I don't have any shoes that would fit you," she apologized, handing me a bundle. She sat down beside Wiesmulluer, looking up at him with a glow in her eyes. "You know, I'm not in the habit of providing horses and clothes to every Tom, Dick, and Harry that comes down the pike," she said, hitching her chair closer to his.

Wiesmulluer dropped his spoon, hitching his chair away and looking nervously around the room. "As we explained, madam, we have been robbed. We have no money to pay you with."

"Oh, please, call me Bertha," she said, creeping closer as Wiesmulluer gulped his coffee. "As far as payment goes, money wasn't what I had in mind."

Old man Wiesmulluer choked, spitting coffee across the room, his face turning red as a sunset. "Madam, please," he stuttered, looking at me for help, but if he thought I was jumping into this one, he was loco as a crazed hog.

"Come on, sugar. I said, call me Bertha. There's no need to be formal, especially since we are going to be close. Real close," she cooed, leaning her head on his shoulder and running her fingers up and down his arm. "My, you certainly are a big, strapping man."

Even from across the table, I could hear Wiesmulluer swallow. ''We could bring your payment back. Once we catch the thieves,'' Wiesmulluer said, pulling his handkerchief and mopping his forehead. ''We would, of course, return your belongings,'' he added, his words ending in a yelp. I swear, he jumped a mile in the air as Bertha laid her hand on his leg.

Grinning into my coffee cup, I let out a snicker and received a vicious kick under the table. Glowering at that old man, I rubbed my leg and kept quiet.

Wiesmulluer straightened up in his chair and slapped a dignified look on his face. ''That's what we will do. As soon as we catch these men, we'll bring your stuff back.''

''Oh, posh, that sounds like a terrible bother,'' Bertha said, pulling him back down in his chair. ''If your young friend wants to go saddle the horses, we could talk about other arrangements.''

All my life, I thought old man Wiesmulluer was the toughest, meanest man alive. I woulda swore there wasn't nothing in the world that could put fear into him, but I was wrong. A look of pure terror on his face, he shot to his feet, his chair skittering across the floor.

''We gotta go!'' he screamed. Her grabbed his bundle of clothes and bolted for the door.

''Humph,'' Bertha grunted, her shoulders slumping as she slapped the table. For a second, she stared at the scarred tabletop, her lower lip sticking out as she pouted.

Right then, I didn't know what to do, but I knew I didn't want to be left here alone with that woman. I reached cautiously for my clothes. My hand froze as Bertha's head came up, her eyes boring into me. All of a sudden, her eyes brightened and a smile grew on her face. She licked her fingers, then touched her hair. "Perhaps, you . . ."

Maybe she said more. I reckon she did, but I didn't hear it. I shot outta my chair and across the room like I'd been zapped in the seat by a bolt of lightning. Ignoring the pain in my bare feet, I skedaddled across the yard and ducked inside the barn. Wiesmulluer was already saddling his horse, not even bothering to look up as I burst in.

Not wanting to be left here alone, I opened a stall and led a mangy bay horse out. Glancing about the barn, I didn't see another saddle. By that time, Wiesmulluer was ready to leave, and believe me, he wasn't in the mood to wait around. Right then, I decided I could do without a saddle. I slipped a crusty old bridle on my horse and jumped on his back.

As we rode by, Bertha stood on the porch shaking her fist and cursing us mightily. "Come back here, you ungrateful curs!" she shouted.

We didn't stop. No, sir, not until we were a good mile away from the place. Then Wiesmulluer stopped.

He leaned back in the saddle and sucked in air like a camel with consumption.

"What the devil was that all about?" he asked between gasps. He shook his head, looking both confused and amused.

Trying my best not to burst out laughing, I shook my head. "I think she was sweet on you, sugar!" I said as a snicker snuck out of my mouth.

For a second, I thought I'd pushed him too far. That old man had a bear trap of a temper, and believe me, when it snapped shut on your backside, it took more than hide.

Gulping, I took a step back, afraid he'd blow his top. All of a sudden, he busted up laughing, slapping his thigh. "Man, I thought we were gonna have to shoot our way outta there," he said, shuddering a little as he wiped his brow.

Nodding in agreement, I started to turn my horse to pick up the trail, but Wiesmulluer stopped me. "Listen, Teddy, let's not tell anyone what just happened." That old man gave me an oily grin and held out his hand. "Once you and Eddy get married, we are to be buddies, so we could keep this our little secret. No reason why Marie would ever have to find out about this."

Toying with my reins, I looked away, not wanting to meet his eyes. This was just too good of a story to keep under my hat.

"Please, Teddy," Wiesmulluer pleaded.

"Yes, sir, Mr. Wiesmulluer, I'll try to keep it quiet," I said, then added hastily, " 'course, if someone was to ask me about it, I'd have to tell the truth."

"Why?" Wiesmulluer demanded, grabbing my arm with his beartrap grip. "You could just make up a story."

"Lying ain't never right," I said, trying to leave myself an out. This was too good of a story to keep. "But if nobody asks, I won't say a word," I finally promised.

Wiesmulluer smiled from ear to ear, slapping me on the back. "Good, boy. Look, why don't you call me Karl. After all, soon as you and Edwinia finally get around to getting married, we'll be family."

"Yes, sir . . . I mean sure, Karl," I said, relieved that he didn't ask me to call him Dad. I don't know if I woulda been able to stomach that.

"All right then, let's go get our stuff back," he said, whacking me across the shoulders again.

We picked up the trail with no problems, moving along at a good clip. My spirits climbed as we closed the gap. Right then, I was looking forward to getting my boots back.

An hour later, the rain started.

We looked at the sky, cursing our luck. Thirty minutes later, we were soaked through to the skin and the trail was a memory. I wanted to stop, but that old man would have none of it. He kept at it even after the tracks faded to nothing.

Finally, even the hardbitten Wiesmulluer had to give up. We spent a miserable night huddled in the scant protection of a canyon wall, without even the luxury of a fire. Wiesmulluer grumbled and cussed the night long as the pelting rain finally slacked off into a drizzle.

Morning came bright and brilliant, holding the promise of a beautiful day. The day may have looked good, but my mood wasn't. I hadn't slept well on the rough, wet ground. I was stiff and rough as a washboard, but as bad as I felt, I knew it was better than Karl. He came off the ground cracking and popping like an overloaded wagon.

"Are you okay," I asked, wincing as his joints snapped.

A flicker of irritation streaked across his whiskered face. "I'm fine," he growled, moving to his horse. "Let's get going."

I kinda thought we'd be heading into Miles City, but it wasn't to be. Instead, we roamed the hills, looking for any sign of them kids. Come nightfall, we hadn't even seen a turkey track, and Wiesmulluer wasn't fit to live with.

Another night on the cold ground didn't improve his mood or his looks. His face was red and covered with whiskers, his white hair looking like a bird's nest.

"Let's head into town. Maybe we can find the others," he reluctantly said through tight lips.

"I hope they haven't run into trouble. They should have caught up to us by now," I observed.

"They better not be lounging in the saloon," Wiesmulluer said, and from the sound of his voice I knew he'd have their hides if he found out they stopped for even one drink.

The whole way to town, Wiesmulluer never said a word . . . well, none that I could repeat anyway. We pulled up just outside Miles City. "Seems to be a busy place," I commented, looking at the mob of people gathered in the street.

"Yeah," Wiesmulluer agreed sullenly. "You'd think them fools would have work to do," he added, kicking his horse into motion.

As we rode slowly down the street, Bertha stepped out of the crowd, pointing an angry finger at us. "That's them!" she screamed with enough windpower to move a clipper ship.

More than a little taken back by the way the snarling mob jumped at us, we jerked our horses to a stop. That was a big mistake—we shoulda cut and run. "What the devil?" Wiesmulluer muttered, echoing my own sentiments.

"Stand back," a big bearded man roared, holding the crowd back with a hairy arm. "I'll handle this."

The big man took a step toward us, then stopped, setting his feet squarely under him. He drew a pistol and pointed it square at Karl. Without a word, he drew back the hammer.

Chapter Two

Pure hate shinning in his eyes, the big man took a step at us, looking down the barrel of his gun. "I'm gonna kill you, mister!"

"Now, hold on a minute. There must be some mistake," I yelled, hoping to reason with this man, which was a dreadful mistake.

"Don't listen to them, Abner. They're trying to make a fool of you!" Bertha screamed.

Now, I reckon making a fool out of Abner wouldn't be the hardest trick in the world to turn. His face strained red and his eyebrows scrunched up as he thought it over. Suddenly, he looked at me, the muzzle of that gun following his eyes. "Who are you?" he demanded.

"Teddy Cooper. I'm—"

"Never heard of you," Abner said truculently. He spat in the dirt and jabbed that pistol at me like it was a lightning rod or something. "You with him?" he demanded.

I took one look at that gun and knew what I had to do. "Never seen him before," I declared, edging my horse sideways.

Now, I mighta made it, but that danged old Wiesmulluer grabbed my bridle, pulling my horse back. "Get back here!" he hissed.

A candle musta flickered somewhere in Abner's weak brain, 'cause his face lit up. "So, you are together!" he said.

"I told you they was," Bertha said, smacking him across the shoulders. "Now shoot them."

"Hold it!"

As the harsh challenge echoed in our ears, a tall man with a big, black mustache strode into the street carrying a shotgun. It wasn't the shotgun or the mustache which caught my eye. No sir, it was the shiny badge pinned to his chest.

"Finally, somebody with brains," Wiesmulluer grunted.

"Shut up. Nobody's talking to you," the sheriff snapped, slapping Wiesmulluer with a severe look. "Abner, what is going on here?" the sheriff asked, holding the shotgun across his chest.

"Stay out of this, Len. There's nothing here to concern you," Abner said, challenging Len's icy stare.

‘‘If you are fixin’ to kill this man, it concerns me a great deal. Now, what exactly is going on around here?’’

‘‘He stole my horses!’’ Bertha said, stepping forward. She pointed a shaky finger at Wiesmulluer. ‘‘The old geezer took advantage of my hospitality. Then he stole my horses!’’

‘‘Huh?’’ Len asked, scratching the side of his jaw with the barrel of the shotgun. ‘‘What do you mean?’’

Bertha cut her eyes toward the ground and traced a line in the dirt with her shoe. ‘‘I don’t want to say in front of everybody. Let’s just say, he got a little too friendly.’’

‘‘What!’’ Wiesmulluer screamed, his voice thundering like a herd of buffaloes. ‘‘Why, you crazy old bat,’’ he growled, and took a step at her.

Abner snapped his gun up, ready to plug ol’ Wiesmulluer. ‘‘Abner!’’ Sheriff Len shouted, stepping between them. ‘‘Put that gun away. There’ll be no killing here today.’’

Abner hunched his shoulders and planted his feet firmly in the dusty street. ‘‘He insulted Bertha,’’ he maintained, crossing his arms. ‘‘Her honor must be defended!’’ he declared and received a rousing roar of support from the crowd. Abner grinned, looking back at the crowd. ‘‘I ain’t gonna kill him. I’m just gonna rough him up a little.’’

A look of doubt crossed the sheriff's face. Finally, he gave into the urging of the crowd and stepped back. Whooping loudly, Abner advanced at Wiesmulluer.

"Crawl off that horse, you old scarecrow. I'm gonna brand your skinny behind with the sole of my boot!"

Now, on his best day, Wiesmulluer ain't an easy-going sort of man. But today, after all we'd been through, he was rough as a mile of bad road. Without a word, he threw down his reins and jumped from his horse, ready to meet the challenge.

Abner jumped in the air, waving his arms and kicking his heels. "I'm gonna peel your hide and nail it to the barn. I'm gonna gouge out your eyes. Then I'm gonna break your legs!" Still shouting, Abner beat his chest and slapped his own face.

While Abner paced back and forth, working himself into a froth, the townsfolk begin placing their bets. As I watched them, an idea began to cook in my head. You see, we were dead broke and we needed money in the worst way.

A tall, ladder-thin man with an Adam's apple that looked like he swallowed a banana sideways waved a handful of money over his head, trying desperately to place a bet on Abner, but he wasn't finding any takers. Hesitation creeping on me, I glanced at Karl. Right then, he looked mad enough and mean enough to whip the world, and we needed the money.

"You're covered," I shouted at the thin man.

His mouth falling open, Wiesmulluer lowered his hands, turning to gape at me. "Look out!" I shouted, but it was too late.

Spying the opening, Abner attacked. His big fist smashed Wiesmulluer in the face, knocking the older man sideways. Seizing the advantage, Abner pummeled poor old Wiesmulluer with heavy blows, driving him to his knees.

While Karl sat on his hands and knees, shaking the cobwebs out of his head, Abner beat his chest and threw his hands to the sky. As the crowd roared their approval, Abner drew back a huge boot, ready to deliver the knockout blow. Abner thought Wiesmulluer was finished, but he didn't know that old man.

When Abner drew his leg back, Wiesmulluer threw himself into Abner's support leg. Bellering like a wounded rhino, Abner toppled to the ground. Wiesmulluer didn't press his advantage, choosing to use the time to catch his breath.

The two of them climbed to their feet, circling each other as they sized one another up. His arms held wide, Abner let out a roar and charged. The quicker of the two, Wiesmulluer jumped sideways, tripping the bigger man. As the big man flew past him, Wiesmulluer pasted him in the ear. Letting out a bloodcurdling howl, Abner plowed nosefirst into the street.

Quick as a wink, Wiesmulluer spun around, launching a mighty kick. That kick whacked Abner in the head with an awful crunch. Now, it wasn't Abner's hard head that crunched; no, sir, it was Wiesmulluer's bare foot.

A beller roared out of Wiesmulluer's mouth as he hopped around on one foot, holding his injured toes. A grin spreading across his face, Abner bounced to his feet. He hauled off and popped Wiesmulluer in the mouth and from there on out the fight was pretty much over. With relentless punches, Abner battered the old man to the ground. You had to hand it to Wiesmulluer, he tried to get up, but he just didn't have it left in him.

As Wiesmulluer melted back to the ground, I felt the skinny man's eyes boring into me. Sneaking a peek over my shoulder, I saw him bearing down on me. ''You owe me twenty bucks,'' he crowed and stuck his hand out.

I coulda kicked myself. I shoulda cut and run once I saw Wiesmulluer was beat, or better yet, I should've kept my mouth shut and never made the bet. Deciding to see if I could reason with the man, I splattered a big grin across my face and turned to face him. ''A funny thing just happened. You see, I have a tiny problem.''

''I don't give a hoot or holler about your problems. All I want is my money,'' the man said.

I smiled again, looking out of the corner of my eyes for my horse and cursing myself for dismounting. ''You see the money is the problem.''

The skinny man stepped up to me, bumping his chest against mine. ''You better not be trying to say you don't have the money.''

''W-e-l-l,'' I said, spreading my hands in front of me.

That scrawny feller snarled and balled his fist. For just a second, I thought he was gonna take a poke at me. I reckon he finally got around to noticing that while he was tall, I stood a mite higher and a bunch broader. Instead of taking a swipe at me, he turned and hollered at the sheriff.

''Quit your caterwauling, Weeb,'' Sheriff Len said, his voice cutting through Weeb's squawkin'. His face cold, the sheriff looked across at me, his finger finding the trigger of that shotgun. ''We frown on welshers in these parts. You wouldn't be thinking about running out on a debt, now, would you?''

''No, no,'' I said hurriedly. ''It's just that I don't have the money on me,'' I explained lamely.

''You shoulda had that in mind when you made the bet, you big oak tree,'' Weeb declared.

You know, I had just about took all the yapping from him that I could stand. I took a step at him, but he scooted behind the sheriff, and I found myself staring down the muzzle of the sheriff's gun.

''Pick up your friend and carry him over to the jail,'' Len instructed.

''The jail? What for?'' I asked.

"He's been accused of stealing horses," Sheriff Len explained. He shot a look at Bertha, then added solemnly. "Among other things."

With the crowd hooting and hollering at us, I helped Karl to his feet. With one arm around his waist, I half drug the old man over to the jail. As we reached the jail, the sheriff reached around me and opened the door. "The cells are in the back. Just keep going."

There were two cells in the back. One of them was occupied with men sleeping in the bunks. Hardly sparing them a glance, I carried Wiesmulluer into the empty cell. As I placed him in a bunk, I heard the cell door slam shut.

"Hey!" I shouted, almost tripping as I whirled around. "What are you locking me up for? Bertha said he was the one that took the horses," I declared, conveniently forgetting to own up to my part in taking the mounts. The way I seen it, if Bertha thought I didn't need to be drug into this, that was her business. Anyway, there wasn't no need in both of us being in jail.

"That she did," Sheriff Len acknowledged and smiled. "But you just welshed on a bet. That's a crime in these parts. A very serious crime."

"Hey! You wanna keep it down? We're trying to sleep over here," a sleepy voice called from the next cell.

I spun around, ready to tell that yahoo to shut his yap and mind his own business, but as the man rolled over and sat up, the words hung in my craw. My mouth fell plumb down to my knees as I recognized the man. Bobby Stamper!

Chapter Three

"What are you doing here?" we both shouted at the same time.

"They claim we robbed their bank," Bobby answered with a wry shake of his head.

"And what makes them think that?" I asked suspiciously. Bobby smiled, cocking his head to look at the sheriff, who was listening to our conversation with great interest. "We was walking along when we happened on five horses just standing in this canyon. Them horses were lathered up and tuckered out, but we figured they'd beat walking. We'd just got mounted up when the good sheriff showed up." Stamper finished his story with a smile and a small salute for Sheriff Len. I swear, for a man in jail he sure seemed happy.

''What are you grinnin' about?'' I asked sourly, and had to jump to catch Wiesmulluer as the old coot pitched out of his cot.

Stamper shrugged, changing the subject. ''What happened to Karl? Is he going to be all right?'' he asked, as Preacher Tom and Mr. Claude sat up in their bunks.

I leaned Wiesmulluer back against the wall, making sure he wouldn't fall again before I answered. ''He got himself into a small dispute with a gentleman in the street.''

''What happened to you two? Did you catch them kids and get our stuff back?'' Louis Claude asked.

I shook my head sadly. ''No, we couldn't catch them on foot.''

''How come you two are in jail? What did you do?'' Preacher Tom wanted to know.

''It's a long story,'' I said, but thinking back on what happened, I decided it was one I wanted to tell. I scuffed my toe and wrung my hands, but no matter how hard I tried, I couldn't hold that story back. It just sorta busted out of me in a rush.

A smile on my face, I crossed to the bars that divided the two cells. ''You ain't gonna believe this,'' I said, looking back at Wiesmulluer to make sure he wasn't listening. He wasn't. He just stared blankly at the wall. Stifling a snicker, I told them the story.

''So, the old dog can still hunt,'' Bobby observed, sporting a leering grin.

Before I could think of a response to that, the sheriff stepped up to the bars, looking at me with a curious expression. ''You say you were all on your way to buy cattle and were robbed by a bunch of kids?'' he asked, and I nodded.

''That's what we've been trying to tell you,'' Preacher Tom shouted, leaping up to the bars. ''These men are honest, respected cattlemen from Whiskey City, Wyoming. I am the town minister.''

Sheriff Len lifted an eyebrow, taking in Preacher Tom's wild hair and huge wad of chewing tobacco. ''You are a preacher?''

''You bet your slop bucket I am,'' Preacher Tom declared, glaring fiercely at the sheriff. ''Why, Teddy here is the sheriff of our town.''

Sheriff Len paced back and forth, rubbing his jaw. ''Is that right?'' he asked, a note of doubt in his tone.

''They kinda forced the job on me. I was a rancher, but a snowstorm killed my cattle, and then all my crops died. The town needed a sheriff, and I needed a job,'' I said, with a shrug.

''I didn't ask for your life story,'' the sheriff growled.

''Surely, you don't still believe that we had anything to do with your bank getting robbed?'' Preacher Tom asked hopefully.

''Well, maybe. Your stories do match up,'' the sheriff said, hesitation sounding in his voice. He pointed a finger at Bobby. ''But you are traveling with a known bank robber.''

''Hey, nobody ever caught me robbing a bank,'' Bobby countered, and gave the sheriff a confident smile. ''Besides, I've given all that up. I'm a married, settled man now.''

''Yeah, I bet,'' Sheriff Len said and grunted. Rubbing his jaw, he paced back and forth in front of the cells. ''Still, you didn't have the money with you,'' he muttered. He stopped pacing and stared at us for a long time. ''You boys just hang tight. I'll be back.''

After he left, I stretched out on a bunk. I figured if I was going to be locked up in jail, the least I could do was catch up on my sleep. That bunk wasn't very soft, but after the places I'd been sleeping the last few days, it felt like lying in a mound of feathers.

Shadows stretched across the cell when I woke up. With a big yawn, I sat up, looking around the cell. Wiesmulluer sat on the edge of his bunk, his head down as he rubbed the knot on his jaw. ''You all right?'' I asked.

''Yeah,'' he answered tiredly. ''I'm sorry I let you down, Teddy. I guess I'm getting too old. I reckon I'll have to leave all the roughhousing to you kids.''

As the old man hung his head again, I looked about the cell. My mind searched for the words to make him feel better. ''You done all right. If I hadn't distracted you, you might have won.''

"If you two have finished catching up, maybe we could get out of here," Bobby called from the next cell.

"Get out?" I asked hopefully. "The sheriff has decided to let us go?"

"Sure, he must have or else he woulda put better locks on these doors." Bobby flashed me a grin, then hit the cell door with the palm of his hand. To my surprise, the door swung open.

Bobby started to step through, but Preacher Tom grabbed him by the shoulder and hauled him back. "Just a minute. Breaking out of jail and fleeing from the law is a sin."

"The Lord helps those who help themselves," Bobby reminded him. "The way I see it, if we want to get out of this mess, we'll have to find the men who robbed the bank and bring them in to the sheriff."

"You think we can do this?" Mr. Claude asked, a glimmer of hope ringing in his voice.

"Sure," Bobby assured. "I gotta good idea where to look."

"Sounds good to me," Wiesmulluer said, grunting as he climbed to his feet. "Let's get going." I tell you, for a man that was down in the dumps just a second ago, he was sure full of fire and vinegar now.

"I don't know," Preacher Tom worried. He looked at me. "What do you think, Teddy?"

Now, to be downdog truthful, I wasn't at all sure that busting out of jail was the right thing to do, but it beat anything I could come up with. ''Get us out of here.''

Wearing a mile-long grin, Bobby pulled a small piece of wire from his boot top and went to work on the lock on our cell door. ''Now you're talking,'' he said and in less than two shakes he opened our door.

Pushing past Bobby, I hurried to the guncase beside the sheriff's desk. ''I reckon if we are going to catch the jaspers that really robbed the bank for the sheriff, the least he can do is furnish us some guns to do the job with.''

''Give me one of those pistols,'' Bobby said, reaching around me. There was only two pistols, so I gave him one and kept the other for myself.

''You want a gun, Tom?'' I asked as I gave a rifle to Karl and Mr. Claude.

''Vengeance is mine, saith the Lord,'' Preacher Tom quoted. ''But I don't reckon he'll mind a little help with this one,'' he added, jerking a rifle from the rack.

''All right. Let's get going, then,'' I said, leading the way to the door. At the door I pulled the curtain back and checked the street. By now, the sun had slid out of sight and darkness settled on the land. I couldn't see much in the dark, but the street appeared deserted.

My hand on the doorknob, I glanced back at my friends. ''Everybody ready?'' I asked, and received a nod from every man. I opened the door a crack and poked my head outside. I was just about to jump out when I saw a terrifying sight waddling up the street.

"Yikes!" I yelled, pulling my head back inside and slamming the door. "Get back in the cell."

Instead of running for the cells, the whole bunch of them crowded up to the window, nearly crushing me in the process. "What is it? Is the sheriff coming back?" Bobby asked, straining to look over my shoulder.

"Worse!" I shouted. "It's Bertha coming with a big tray of food."

"Bertha?" Wiesmulluer howled. "Get outta my way!" he shouted. In his haste he ran smooth over poor Mr. Claude and shoved Preacher Tom up against the wall. Muttering under his breath, he scrambled back into our cell. He grabbed the door and woulda pulled it shut, if I hadn't dove and grabbed the door with both hands.

"I gotta get in there too," I shouted, pulling back on that door with all my might. I guess that didn't matter to him, 'cause he set his feet and fought to pull it shut.

Bobby and Preacher Tom jumped in to help me and finally tore the door from his grasp. As the others scooted into their cell, I leaped into mine, jerking the door shut behind me.

"The guns!" Mr. Claude shouted. "We must hide the guns."

In a whirlwind of motion, we ripped the guns off and stuffed them under the grass mattresses of the bunks. We barely completed the job, when Bertha breezed into the office.

She gave us a cheery smile and placed the heavy tray on the desk. ''I thought you boys might be getting hungry,'' she said, her rough, red face practically glowing.

A dazed look on his face, Preacher Tom stepped to the bars. He grinned back at her and commenced to mashing his hair down. ''That was most kind of you, ma'am.''

Bertha took a plate off the tray, paying Preacher Tom no mind. She carried the plate over to our cell, her eyes glued to Wiesmulluer as she set the plate on the floor. Grinning coyly, she touched her hair. ''How about it, sugar, are you hungry?'' Lowering her eyes, she pulled up her skirt, showing her leg over the top of her laceup shoes. Using the toe of her shoe, she nudged the plate under the bars. ''Eat up, sugar, you need to keep your strength up. After you get out, I have plans for you.''

For a second, Wiesmulluer didn't move; he just stared at her, his mouth hanging open. All of a sudden, he roared. ''Get out!'' He launched a mighty kick at the plate and would have kicked the plate over except that I snatched it out of his reach. I'm an eating man and hated to see good food go to waste.

Missing his kick, Wiesmulluer had to grab the bars to keep his balance. Bertha grabbed his hand, patting it lightly. Old man Wiesmulluer jerked away from her touch like it was a branding iron. ‘‘Leave me alone,’’ he ranted. ‘‘You’re the reason I’m in here!’’

‘‘Karl! That’s not a very Christian attitude,’’ Preacher Tom scolded harshly. ‘‘This kindly woman is only trying to help.’’

‘‘Why, thank you, sir,’’ Bertha cooed. She glanced at Tom out of the corner of her eye and gave him a little wave, then turned back to Wiesmulluer. ‘‘I’m dreadfully sorry about getting you in trouble, sugar. You upset me. I guess I just lost my head.’’

‘‘If you ask me, it wasn’t much of a loss,’’ Wiesmulluer grumbled, turning away from the bars. ‘‘Now, if you’d just get lost, I’d be happy.’’

‘‘Well, I never!’’ Bertha fumed. With a snap of her skirts she whirled around and flounced out of the jail.

‘‘That certainly wasn’t very nice,’’ Preacher Tom snapped, searing old man Wiesmulluer with a burning look.

‘‘Never mind that,’’ Bobby said, his lock pick ready. ‘‘We got things to do.’’

While Bobby opened the two locks, I tore into that plate of food. By the time he had the doors open, I had it almost slicked up. I coulda ate more, but the others didn’t show any interest in the food. They were far more interested in getting out of town.

This time, we made it down to the stable without incident. "You fellers get us some horses," I said, then sprinted back down the alley.

I stopped at the back door of the general store, hesitating as I fought my conscience. Setting my jaw firm, I kicked open the door. Fumbling around in the dark, I banged and barked my knees before I found a stack of jeans. I scraped five pairs off the top and stuck them under my arm, then I hurried over to the boots. I selected five pairs, then left an IOU for the clerk. Gathering my stuff, I snuck back to the stable. Minutes later, under a bright, full moon, we rode slowly and silently out of town, slipping through the shadows like five ghosts.

Several miles from town, the first rays of light hit us as we huddled in a makeshift camp. "We should go back to where we were arrested and pick up the trail of the real thieves," Mr. Claude suggested.

"No good," I said, shaking my head. "It's rained since then. All the tracks would be gone."

"What should we do? We can't simply roam around and hope to find them," Preacher Tom wailed.

"I can find them," Bobby said, his voice quietly confident.

"How?" Wiesmulluer said with a growl, the bruises on his face making him look meaner than ever.

Bobby grinned, pointing northwest with his arm. "There's a hideout back in the hills where most of the boys go to lay low after they've pulled a job. I figure the men we are after went there."

Wiesmulluer's eyebrows shot up; he grumbled under his breath and spat on the ground. "Funny that you should know of this place. I suppose you been there?"

"A time or two," Bobby admitted cheerfully.

Wiesmulluer glared at Bobby. I don't reckon that old man had gotten used to the fact that his daughter married an outlaw. He had some more to say, but I beat him to it. "The sheriff's probably on our tail already. We ain't got time to argue. Let's go get 'em," I urged, ready to get this over with.

Stamper shook his head emphatically. "Are you loco? That isn't a place you can just waltz into."

I scratched my head. "You were the one that said we should bust out of jail and catch these guys."

Stamper shrugged and gave me an infuriating grin. "I just said that so you all would come with me. I don't like being behind bars."

"You're an outlaw. Can't you get us into this place?" Preacher Tom asked.

"Get us in?" Bobby asked, lifting an eyebrow. "Getting in will be dead dog easy compared to getting back out. If them boys ever found out that we weren't what we claimed to be, they'd kill us out of hand."

Well, that convinced me. My enthusiasm for the project melted like a snowball in Lucifer's pantry.

'Course, it never fazed Wiesmulluer any. "Makes no never mind. We got a job to do," he barked, and kicked his horse into motion.

"Whoa, hang on a minute. Don't you think this is something we should talk about?" I stammered.

"No," Wiesmulluer said, without slowing or even turning around.

Cursing, I slapped the saddlehorn and looked to the sky. "Dang, stubborn, old goat. I got a notion to rope and hogtie him till he comes to his senses."

"Now, Teddy, think about it. What would you have us do?" Mr. Claude asked softly. He reached across the saddle, grabbing my forearm. "Karl and I are too old to be running from the law. The reverend too."

"I ain't as old as you!" Preacher Tom declared, then his expression softened. "Of course, a man in my line of work can't be in jail; it tends to put off the parishioners."

"And think about you and Bobby. Bobby just got married and you're about to. You don't want to start off your lives like this," Mr. Claude reasoned, and gave my arm a squeeze.

"Well, if you put it thataway . . . ," I stammered. "Still, I don't reckon being dead is any picnic either." I looked to Bobby, who shrugged and spread his hands. "Well, we could go take a gander at the place. If the odds seem too high, we could back out."

"That's the spirit," Mr. Claude said.

Well, I can't say that I had the spirit, but I followed along. For hours, Stamper led us through a maze of twisting canyons. We rode slow, winding between the boulders that littered the canyon floor.

Wiesmulluer opened his canteen and glared at Bobby. "Are you sure you know where you're going?" he said, growling. He poured water from the canteen on his bandanna and washed the back of his neck.

Bobby yawned and scratched the stubble on his cheeks. "We're almost there," he promised and turned into a small offshoot.

The walls of this canyon squeezed so close together that a man could almost stretch his arms and touch both sides. I stood in the stirrups and peered over Bobby's shoulder. I could see that the canyon widened as it cut through the rocks, but not much.

Bobby took off his hat and stood up in the stirrups. "Oh yeah, this is the place," he said.

Looking around, I didn't like it. The canyon gave me the creeps; I could almost feel the walls closing. This was a perfect place for an ambush. Without thinking, I touched my pistol, just to make sure I still had it.

"We're home free now," Bobby called, still standing in the stirrups. A second later a rifle shot ripped through the still air, tossing Bobby from the saddle.

Chapter Four

Even as Bobby hit the ground, the rest of us dove out of our saddles. As the others scrambled to cover, I lunged toward Bobby, intent on pulling him to safety. I was still three feet away from him when another bullet hit the ground right in front of me. That bullet kicked up a sandstorm, showering my face and stinging my eyes. Blinded, I grabbed at my eyes and rolled over, trying to find protection.

"Throw down your guns and come out with your hands up," an eerie voice echoed from up the canyon.

Rubbing my smarting eyes, I looked to where Bobby lay, his body crumpled on the trail. Even though he appeared as only a bleary, fuzzy lump, I could tell he wasn't moving.

A burst of murderous anger surged up inside of me. Throw down my gun? Not hardly. If this jasper wanted to play rough, I'd show him a thing or two. Nobody shot down one of my friends!

With a last look at Bobby, I drew my gun, ready to leap out and gun down our attacker like the dirty dog he was.

"I said throw down your guns!" To punctuate his order, the drygulcher fired a warning shot. The bullet smacked into the rocks above our heads, ricocheting wildly. On the second bounce, the bullet struck the sand right in front of Bobby's head. Surprisingly, he flinched. Not only that, a second later he jumped to his feet. And let me tell you, for a dead man he bounced up real good too.

"Chub, you idiot! Knock that off!" he screamed.

Silence cascaded down over the canyon. Our attacker raised his head, calling out in a hushed voice. "Bobby? Is that you?"

"Who in blazes did you think it would be?" Bobby snapped, irritation riding in his voice. "Now stop all the shooting before you hurt somebody."

I raised up to my knees, rubbing my eyes. I wondered if that spray of sand messed them up, 'cause I wasn't sure what I was seeing. "I thought you was dead," I whispered.

"Not hardly," Bobby grumped. "He shot a foot over my head, but I figured it would be best to play dead, till I figured out who was on guard duty."

"You knew they would shoot at us?" Mr. Claude said accusingly. Bobby flashed him a grin, then ducked his head. "Yeah, I reckon I did. I just forgot." Bobby bent down to pick up his hat, then strolled up the canyon to meet Chub, who labored mightily as he climbed down from his nest of rocks.

"Danged fool," Wiesmulluer muttered, matching my own sentiments exactly.

Hands on hips, I studied Chub. He was a little, rat-like man with buck teeth and quick, nervous movements. Blowing out a big sigh, I snatched my hat off the ground and clapped it on my head. Right then my temperature was shooting through the roof, and I was sore as a blood blister. I don't rightly know who I was the maddest at—Chub for shooting at us, or Bobby for playing dead.

"I guess we are in now," Mr. Claude observed as Bobby and Chub shook hands like old friends. They laughed and whacked each other on the back. Still laughing, Bobby turned, waving for us to follow them.

Preacher Tom looked to the sky. "God, help us now," he asked.

"Yeah," Wiesmulluer agreed grimly. He checked his rifle, then gathered his reins. Without a word, he led his horse after them.

"Let's go," I told the others. I took the reins to my horse and Bobby's, my feet reluctantly leading me along.

The walk wasn't a long one. The canyon wound around a couple of times, then suddenly opened into a large cul-de-sac. The cul-de-sac was roughly a hundred yards each way. Brown, tough-looking grass covered the valley floor, and smooth rock walls stretched straight up a hundred feet. A cluster of buildings sat at the far end. They looked shabby and out of place in this wild, beautiful setting.

A group of men stood in front of the buildings, holding their weapons ready as they studied us. A hulk of a man stepped away from the group, advancing grimly toward us. He walked slowly, his thumbs hooked in his gunbelt. His shirt hung open, revealing a huge, muscled chest. He stopped a few yards from us, staring at us through slitted eyes.

"Riley," Stamper said curtly.

"What are you doing here, Stamper?" Riley demanded.

"Just looking for a place to hole up for a few days," Bobby replied, with a casual shrug.

"What made you think you would be welcome here?"

"What makes you think I care?" Bobby countered.

Like two bulls, they glared at each other, neither willing to give an inch. I licked my lips, knowing trouble was riding up on us. Moving slowly, I flipped the thong off my pistol and took a couple of steps to my right, wanting to give myself a better angle to fire.

"Come on, guys. We don't need any trouble here," Chub said, nervously tugging at Riley's sleeve. "There's no call for this. Bobby's all right; everybody knows that."

His face stiff with anger, Riley tore away from Chub's clutching fingers. "You just keep out of my way!" Having spoke his piece, he turned and pushed through the crowd.

"Riley Hunt?" I asked, and Bobby nodded grimly. "Well, I can see where his kids got their snooty disposition."

"Yeah," Bobby agreed, absently staring as Hunt walked away. "Stay away from him. Everybody just lay low and let me do all the asking around," Bobby warned under his breath. Planting a smile on his face, Bobby stepped forward to meet the folks. I swear, Stamper knew every man in the place. They laughed and hooted as they whisked him away.

Looking around nervously, we followed along. They led us inside a low log building. A rickety bar ran across the end of the building. That bar didn't look very sturdy, but it held up the big man leaning on it. My eyes widened at the sight of him, and I took a step back. That man could scare the hair off a hog. His head was bald and shiny, his eyes slitted and cold. He stood up to his full height, folding arms the size of redwoods across his chest. When he straightened up, I saw why his head was so bare and shiny; it actually brushed the ceiling.

"Bobby! You little stink bug, where you been keeping yourself?" the man asked, but there was little warmth in either his tone or his expression.

"Oh, here and there," Bobby answered, his voice booming. "Now, are you going to stand there yapping or pour me and my friends a drink? Shoot, pour one for everybody. I'm buying."

Baldy didn't budge an inch. He just stared at Bobby with a guarded eye. "You got any money?"

"Luther!" Bobby called out gleefully. "Since when do I need money in here? Isn't my credit good with you?"

"You still owe me from the last time you was here."

"And I intend to pay you every cent, just as soon as I pull a job. You know I'm good for it."

Luther rubbed his shaven head, eyeing Bobby like a hawk eyes a mouse. "Yeah, and you know I'll break your scrawny neck if you don't," Luther growled, but he started pouring.

"We'll take ours over at the table," Bobby decided, motioning for us to join him at a back table.

"There's a lot of people here. How are we going to find out who robbed the bank in Miles City?" I asked.

Bobby shrugged, pulling back a chair. "Keep your eyes and ears open. If they got money, they'll be buying drinks. These guys like to brag. Who knows, they might just up and tell us."

A beer in hand, Chub wandered over to our table. "Bobby, watch yourself around Riley. He's been making a lot of talk about you. He don't like you much."

"What did you do to this guy Riley?" Wiesmulluer asked.

"Nothing much," Bobby said offhand.

"Nothing?" Chub howled. He slapped his thigh and cut his eyes toward the ceiling. He stood hands on hips, staring at the ceiling, then looked at us and shook his head sadly. "Nothing, he says. Why, it was about the most exciting thing that ever happened around here, that's all."

I laughed, taking a liking to the little man. "Pull up a chair and tell us about it," I invited.

Chub looked around, then sat down as Luther brought our beers to the table. Chub waited until the bartender left, then leaned in, speaking in a hushed voice. "It happened one winter a few years back." Chub sipped his beer, shaking his head. "I swear, that was the worst winter of all time. It snowed all winter and a bunch of the boys were here, holed up until the spring thaw. Well, Riley, he got impatient and went out and pulled a job."

Chub stopped as Bobby stood up. "I'm gonna go catch up with some of the boys," Bobby said.

"Yeah, you do that," Chub said, taking a quick drink. He wiped his mouth, then got back to his story. "Anyway, Riley and a couple of the boys went out to pull a job and they done it. They knocked off a fat bank, then while they was making their getaway, the snow caught them. A big Northerner blew in. Snowed for three days. Riley lost his bearings in the blizzard and they got lost. They ended up wandering around for ten days. Nearly killed them. They was half-dead when they finally stumbled in here. Yes, sir, they was half-dead, but they was five thousand dollars richer.''

Chub drained his beer in one long gulp. Smacking his lips, he slapped the glass down on the table. ''After he got some starch back in his drawers, Riley went to bragging and flashing his money around. One night, him and Bobby got in this big poker game and when it was over, Bobby had all Riley's money.''

Chub looked up as Bobby returned to the table. ''Never in all my born days did I see anybody have such a run of luck. I never could figure out how you done it.''

''I cheated,'' Bobby replied, dropping into his chair. I looked questioningly at him, but he shook his head, then bellowed at the bartender. ''Luther, how about some service?''

A dark expression riding on his face, Luther carried six more mugs to our table. ''You're getting in pretty deep, Bobby. When are you going to pull this job? It's been a long time since you worked.''

''Yeah, we heard you got yourself hitched and settled down,'' Chub said.

''Married? Me?'' Bobby hooted. He leaned across the table, winking broadly. ''Now, I did meet this little gal, but you know, she was just a good-time girl. They ain't made the filly that can trap me.''

Chocking and spitting beer, old man Wiesmulluer shot to his feet. It took all my strength to hold him back. ''While you fellers catch up on old times, me and Karl will go tend the horses.'' I practically had to throw a headlock on the old man and drag him out of the joint. I noticed Luther giving us a funny look, but didn't have time to worry about that, not with Wiesmulluer about to go through the roof.

I finally rassled the old man outside, but he managed to tear away from me. He skidded to a stop, dragging his sleeve across his mouth. ''I'm gonna kill him! Talking about my daughter that way!'' He doubled his fists and stalked toward the door. I nabbed him, pinning him against the wall.

''Now, sir, you know he didn't mean those things. Bobby loves Betsy. You know that.''

Wiesmulluer relaxed and quit screaming in my ear, but I held onto him just the same. Slowly the fire left his eyes and his straining jaw muscles relaxed. ''Maybe,'' he admitted surlily. ''But I still don't like it.''

''Just keep your likes and dislikes to yourself until we get out of here,'' I grumbled. Holding him against the wall with one hand, I picked up his hat and slapped it back on his head. ''We'll be lucky to get out of here alive as it is. We don't need to be fighting among ourselves.''

"All right, you made your point. You don't have to keep yapping about it," he said and pushed me away. A dark look on his face, he started gathering the reins. "I'll tell you one thing, when we get out of here, I'm gonna skob his knob."

"You do that," I said, knowing we hadn't settled anything, just put it off awhile. Most folks would likely forget, but not Wiesmulluer. When it came to being mad and holding a grudge, that old man had the memory of an elephant.

He was still mumbling and muttering as we led the horses into the barn. I looked around the barn, more than a little impressed. While all the other buildings looked to be made outta rawhide and spit, the barn was a solid, well-built structure. I guess men on the run knew the value of keeping their horses in shape.

We were just finishing up when Riley Hunt marched into the barn. One look and I knew he wasn't just observing the social niceties and paying his respects. No, sir, he had something on his mind. He stopped in front of me, crossing his arms and challenging me with an icy stare. "Where did you get them horses?" he demanded.

"What's it to you?" Wiesmulluer asked belligerently.

"Those are the horses we used to rob the bank in Miles City. It seems funny to me that you should have them now. Where did you get them?"

"We stole them," I stammered.

"You're lying," Hunt sneered, whacking me in the chest with the point of his finger. "Who did you steal them from?"

Now, to tell the truth, Riley Hunt scared the bejeebers outta me, but all that jabbing and proddin' he was doing got my dander up. "We don't know who we stole them from," I said, knocking his hand away. "When we rode into Miles City our horses was played out and these were handy, so we took 'em. We didn't ask around as to where they come from."

"You swing a pretty wide loop. If I was you, I'd lay real low and hope I don't decide to kill you," Riley said, his voice soft and menacing.

Well, I heard the menace, but I don't reckon Wiesmulluer did. He sneered at Hunt. "You don't scare us!" he said, and gave me a push at Hunt. "Tell him, Teddy."

After that push, I stood jaw to jaw with Hunt, and if I scared him any, he hid it awfully well. He laughed, took the cigar out of his mouth and blew smoke in my face. "You just watch yourself, farmboy. I'm going to be keeping my eye on you." He smiled around the cigar, then whirled and stomped away.

"Why didn't you take him?" Wiesmulluer growled. "He said he was the one that robbed the bank."

"Huh?" I said. I hadn't been paying the old man any mind. To tell the truth, I was still a little shaken. I figured Hunt was the tough dog around here and the thought of tangling with him put a shake in my legs and a pucker in my backside.

"Why didn't you just plug him? We coulda hauled him into town and they woulda had their bank robber."

"He didn't tell us where the money was. Without the money the sheriff would never believe us."

Wiesmulluer hesitated, rubbed the side of his face, and frowned. "Well, that makes no difference. We coulda got the money later," he said, shoving me out the door. "Let's follow him and see where he goes."

Where he went was the saloon. We saw him kick open the saloon door and stomp inside like a man with fire in his britches. "Come on, let's go get the jasper," Wiesmulluer said, and kept pushing me in that direction.

Hunt stood at the bar, his shoulders hunched as he drank. Bobby and the others still sat at our table, and from the looks of things, they were having a high time. Chub laughed at something Bobby said, and that was the wrong thing to do.

Placing his glass carefully on the bar, Hunt turned slowly to face poor Chub. He jerked his cigar out of his mouth, pointing the stogie at Chub. "I thought you was supposed to be on guard duty."

Chub shrank back in his chair, his fingers fiddling with his mug. "I reckon I just forgot in all the excitement. You know, with Bobby showing up and all. I'm real sorry about that, Riley."

Riley threw his cigar down, jumping across the room. "You stupid fool!" he thundered, standing jaw to jaw with Chub. I reckon Chub knew what was coming because he tried to run away but he wasn't quick enough. Riley grabbed the front of Chub's shirt with one hand and pasted the smaller man in the mouth. Blood gushed from Chub's mouth as he tried to beg, but his words came out in a soggy, jumbled mess. A snarl on his lips, Riley hauled back to hit the smaller man again.

I didn't think. There wasn't time. On impulse, I grabbed Hunt's shoulder and spun him around and hit him square on the chops. I'm a big man and put everything I had into that blow. That punch slammed Riley backward, bouncing him off the bar like a poker chip. He hit the floor, but he didn't stay down, not for long anyway. Without a word, he pulled himself to his feet, looking at me with hate in his eyes.

"You're going to regret doing that," he hissed through clenched teeth.

Well, to tell the truth, I already regreted it. Riley Hunt was a big man and I wasn't sure I could whip him, but I reckoned I'd have to try.

I flexed my shoulders and set my feet, ready to meet his charge head on. Hunt didn't rush me. Instead, his hand swooped for his pistol. Too late, I clawed for my own gun, but I knew I'd never get it out in time.

Chapter Five

Hunt's pistol came up as my own stuck in the leather holster. A smile flickering on his lips, he leveled his gun at me. Just when I knew I was a goner, Luther smacked Hunt over the head with a short club.

My knees shook like a loose wheel as Hunt crashed to the floor. I had to swallow a couple of times before I could get any words out of my throat. Even then, they wavered and squeaked a mite. "Thanks, Luther."

Luther waved the club in my direction. "I don't allow no gunplay in here. The blood stains are too hard to scrub off the floor." He frowned, sticking the club back under the bar. "Besides, I'm just protecting my investment. You look like a go-getter to me. Maybe you can get Bobby off his duff and back to work."

"Hey, we're just looking for the right place to hit," Bobby protested.

"There's banks, stages, and mine payrolls. Pick one and rob it so you can pay your bills," Luther growled.

"Well what about you? You haven't pulled a job in years. In fact, nobody can remember the last time you did a job," Bobby countered smugly.

"We ain't talking about me," Luther replied, calmly wiping a damp spot off the bar. "I ain't the one that owes my friends money."

Chub wobbled to the bar, taking a bottle and helping himself to a snort. "Gee, thanks, mister," he stammered, looking wide-eyed at the fallen Hunt.

Cursing under his breath, Luther ripped the bottle from Chub's hand. "Chub, if you know what's good for you, you'll get your scrawny backside out of here and stand your post."

As Chub scurried from the saloon, Luther slammed the bottle down on the bar, glaring fiercely at me. "And unless you want to tangle with Riley, you better make yourself scarce. He's going to be looking for you when he wakes up."

Before any of us knew what was up, Wiesmulluer lunged across the barroom and ripped the pistol from Hunt's limp hand. "Forget that! We're taking him back to Miles City with us," he yelled.

"What?" The cry came from several sets of lips, mine included. While I intended to take Hunt in, I'd

planned to corner him up off by himself. I sure never meant to announce it in the crowded saloon.

For a second nobody moved as silence ruled the saloon. Luther recovered first, his hand racing under the bar for his thumper. "You're the law," he said, brandishing the club and shooting a murderous look at Bobby.

You know, I don't reckon them fellers in that saloon had the slightest interest in us clearing our good names. No, sir, from the cuss words they yelled, I think they were a sight more interested in lynching us. I reckon they mighta done it too, but me and Wiesmulluer had a gun apiece in our fists, and in less than a heartbeat, so did Stamper.

"You boys just sit tight," I warned.

One of them didn't take the warning to heart. He dove sideways out of his chair, his hand clawing at his gun. I tracked him with my gun, but didn't want to shoot. A shot would bring the whole camp down on us, and besides, I didn't want to kill anyone if I didn't have to.

I didn't. Mr. Claude plunked the man over the head with his rifle and that was that. I can tell you, that feller wasn't going to be causing any trouble, not for a day or so.

Luther rested his fists on the bar, gripping that club so tight I thought he was gonna wad it into a ball. "I oughta kill you right now, Bobby Stamper!" he said

through clenched teeth, and I was afraid he'd crawl over the bar and strangle us all. ''You brought the law here!''

''Naw,'' Bobby said in denial, and I'll be danged if he didn't manage a squirrelly grin, which I figured was a mistake. That bartender had arms fit to crush an anvil.

If Bobby feared the huge bartender, he didn't show it. He taunted him with a cocky grin as we herded all the men into a corner.

''We ain't the law. Fact is, we got throwed in jail for robbing the Miles City bank. We busted out, and the only way we can clear ourselves is to take Riley in.''

I crossed behind the bar and took down a stubby shotgun that hung from a set of antlers nailed to the wall. I checked to make sure the gun was loaded, then tossed it to Mr. Claude. ''Watch them,'' I said, nodding my head in the direction of the men grouped in the corner. ''If they so much as blink, give them both barrels.''

Wiesmulluer had already pulled the groggy Hunt to his feet, propping him against the bar. ''Where's the money?'' Wiesmulluer demanded and slapped Riley none too gently in the face. Riley Hunt didn't say a word. He just set his jaw defiantly. ''You better talk, buster, I'm running out of patience,'' Wiesmulluer said threateningly.

"Don't worry, he doesn't have to tell us," Bobby predicted confidently. "Riley here, he never did have any imagination. What did you do with it, Riley? Stuff it under your bunk?"

Riley's mouth dropped open, and a look of panic crossed his face. He recovered mighty quick, but the damage was done. Everybody could see Bobby had hit the nail on the head. Bobby laughed, patting Hunt's face. "You always were dumber than a post."

"You ain't out of here yet," Riley Hunt sneered. "There's forty men in this camp. You don't think they'll just stand by and let you leave."

"Well now, that depends on how popular you are with the boys," I said, jerking Hunt up close to me. I circled my arm around his neck and ground the muzzle of my pistol into his temple. "Anybody tries to stop us and you won't live to see it."

"If I were you, Riley, I'd tell everybody to hang loose," Bobby told him. "Why, it's been a week since Teddy shot anybody, and he's just itching to kill you."

Hunt cursed under his breath, but didn't resist as I drug him over to the door. I held him there as my friends backed away slowly. "We're going to have that shotgun trained on that door," I told the men bunched in the corner. "Anybody even pokes his head out, and we'll cut him in two."

With our guns trained on the bunch, we backed slowly out the door. Hunt seemed to have given up, which should have alerted me that he had an ace up his sleeve.

"You know where his bunk is?" I asked Bobby, who grinned and nodded. "Then get the money. Reverend, you and Karl go get our horses and one for Hunt. Mr. Claude, make sure nobody comes out of the saloon."

They jumped to do as I asked, leaving me and Hunt standing alone in the hard-packed yard. I could feel the hair on the back of my neck stand up and wished they would hurry. I couldn't see anyone, but I couldn't shake the feeling that a hundred guns were trained on my back. Cringing a little, I fought the impulse to scratch the itch between my shoulder blades.

"You'll never get away with this," Hunt said harshly. "Even if you get out of this canyon, my men will track you down and kill you."

"We'll see," I said casually, but deep inside I wondered if he might be right. It was a long way to town.

"I got the money!" Bobby yelled, a pair of saddlebags bouncing on his shoulder as he ran across the yard.

"Go help them with the horses," I hollered, but it was too late. Even as we spoke, Wiesmulluer and the reverend led six horses out of the barn. "Get mounted up. I'll follow you to the opening on foot."

With one arm still around his neck and my pistol pressed against his head, I backed toward the canyon, using Hunt's body as a shield. I figured once we were in the canyon we would have some breathing room. The closer we got to the opening, my spirits rose. I actually begin to think we might pull this off.

Just when I thought we were home free, a man burst from the saloon, cocking a Henry rifle. Whipping my gun around, I snapped a shot at him. I missed by a foot, but the shot was enough to send the man diving for cover. The second I pulled the gun away from his head, Riley Hunt reacted. He smashed his foot down on my toes, then drove his elbow into my stomach.

"Kill them!" Hunt screamed, breaking away from me.

As Hunt twisted away from me, a wave of men poured out of the buildings, swarming like ants out of a kicked hill. I started to curse, but then thought the better of it.

There was a time for cussin', I reckon, but this wasn't it. This was a time for running. Now, I'm a heavy-footed sort of a man, built along the lines of a rhinoceros. Running don't come natural to me, but with bullets kicking up around me, I took off like a leopard.

My friends opened up from the mouth of the canyon, giving me some cover as I ran. Launching myself in a dive, I covered the last ten yards airborne. I hit the ground on all fours, crawling deeper into the canyon.

"Teddy, catch," Wiesmulluer said, tossing me my reins.

My wind whistling in and out of my mouth like a bugle call, I caught the reins and pushed up to my feet. At the mouth of the canyon, Bobby sat on his horse, coolly firing his rifle. From what I could see, he wasn't hitting much, but he was keeping their heads down.

As his rifle ran dry, Bobby whirled his horse. "Let's get out of here," he yelled and slapped the spurs to his horse.

By then, I was in the saddle, giving my own mount a taste of the spurs. Side by side, we pounded down the canyon, weaving through the rocks as we chased our friends. I heard Chub scream at us as we flashed past his post, but couldn't make out his words and I danged sure wasn't going to stop.

Since he knew this part of the country best, Bobby took the lead, and took us on a dizzying chase through the canyons. I rode in the rear, trying to keep an eye on our backtrail, watching for any signs of pursuit. So far, I couldn't see anyone, but I knew they would come. We took ten thousand dollars from them. For that, they would chase us to kingdom come and back. And if they caught us, they'd likely kill us.

The only thing we had going in our favor was that darkness was coming on us. Already in the bottom of the canyons, a gloom began to settle in. I wished Bobby would slow down. Running like this, in the dark and among these boulders, was a good way to break a neck.

"Bobby, slow down," I called; by now he and the others were mere blobs in the dark.

"Just a little farther. I got an idea," he called back, his face a white streak in the gloom.

A second later, he screamed and his face disappeared. "What the . . ."

Too late, I saw the thick rope stretched across the canyon. Before I could react, I rode right into that rope. It struck me a wicked blow in the chest, knocking the wind from my lungs. A second later, I hit the ground and everything went black.

Chapter Six

When I woke, my head felt like a flattened gourd, and when I raised my hands to touch it, I found that my hands were tied. Not only were they tied together, they were lashed to my body.

With my hands tied like that, it was a real struggle just to roll over. Even trying was enough to send waves of pain crashing through my head. When I did finally manage to roll over, what I saw was far worse than the pain in my head.

My friends were stretched out beside me, tied in the same manner as I was. They weren't moving, and I couldn't tell if they were alive or dead. Worried about them, I kicked out with my foot, whacking Wiesmul-luer in the leg.

He grunted and snorted a couple of times, his head lolling back and forth. ‘‘Karl,’’ I hissed.

‘‘What happened?’’ Bobby asked, struggling to sit up.

‘‘You ran us into an ambush. That’s what happened, you danged fool,’’ Wiesmulluer grumbled. He tried to sit up but fell back heavily.

‘‘How come we ain’t dead?’’ Mr Claude asked, sounding groggy as a fog bank.

‘‘Maybe they intend to torture us,’’ Preacher Tom exclaimed.

Well, Preacher Tom was sure enough right. Torture was exactly what was in store for us. Now it wasn’t so much what they were going to do to us, but who was doing it.

It wasn’t Riley Hunt who caught us; it was them good-for-nothing kids. Junior’s face came slowly into my line of sight as the boy leaned over us. ‘‘Where did you get all this money?’’ he asked, shaking the saddlebags over our heads.

‘‘That money doesn’t belong to you, you little heathen. I demand that you give it back and untie us so we can return the money to its rightful owners,’’ Preacher Tom sputtered.

‘‘Shut up, you old coot,’’ the boy said, and smacked the reverend across the head with the saddlebags.

‘‘That money was stolen from the bank in Miles City. They think we did it. We must have the money to take back and prove our innocence,'' Mr. Claude explained, but his words didn't have much effect on Junior.

That boy, I knew there would be no reasoning with him, but maybe one of the girls? The younger one looked as cute and innocent as a newborn fawn, but since she durned near shot me the first time, I didn't waste any time on her. The older girl, she hadn't hardly even spoken. Twisting my neck around until it hurt, I studied her. She had a quiet, serene air about her. Her dark hair fell straight down, framing her face. She was pretty, I decided, with large brown eyes and delicate, sensitive features. She would be the one to reason with.

``Look, young lady. What you are doing here is wrong. Folks are counting on this money to tide them through the winter.'' I could see my words had an effect on her, as she bit her lip and turned away. ``You haven't done anything that we can't fix. Turn us loose and give us back all the money, and we'll help you.''

``Stevie, maybe he is right,'' she pleaded with her brother. ``I don't like any of this.''

``Be quiet, Joan. Get their horses,'' the boy snapped. He turned and kicked me in the side. ``Leave my sister alone!''

``Look, boy. We are in a bind here. We can't afford to lose that money. That's the only thing between us and going to prison,'' Mr. Claude said.

"Well, I guess this just isn't your lucky day," the little creep said, and had the nerve to laugh in our faces. We could still hear them laughing as they mounted up on our horses and rode away.

His face blood red, and a string of cussin' coming out of his mouth, old man Wiesmulluer commenced to flopping around on the ground like a fish out of water.

"When I get loose, I'm gonna hunt them little diaper rats down and flog their backsides raw," he roared.

Watching him rassle against his ropes was like watching a bucking bronco. I swear, it was almost worth all we'd been through just to see the show. By the time he finally got loose, that old man was lathered up like a plow horse. "I made it!" he shouted, wheezing like a pump organ.

"Very good," Bobby said, clapping his hands, "but what took you so long?"

"Huh?" Wiesmulluer grunted, staring stupefied at Bobby. "Why, you little . . . How did you get loose so fast?"

"In my old line of work, you learn to untie a few knots," Stamper answered with a shrug.

"You mean, you actually took time to learn how to get untied?" Mr. Claude asked as Bobby went to work untying the rest of us.

"Naw, not really. But it seems like somebody is always wanting to tie you up."

"I reckon so!" Preacher Tom exclaimed. "Why, we've only been gone from home a few days and already we've been tied up twice."

After Bobby and Wiesmulluer freed the rest of us, we had ourselves a little powwow. We knew from bitter experience that we couldn't catch them kids on foot. Besides, Riley Hunt and his henchmen were looking for us. If they happened on us while we were on foot, we'd be dead ducks. 'Course, if we went back to Miles City, Sheriff Len would toss us back in the clink, and this time, he would make certain we stayed.

The only good thing about this whole deal was, we still had our boots and britches. I considered that a lucky thing.

"I say we forget this whole deal and go home," Mr. Claude said, massaging his wrists.

"No," I said, shaking my head.

"Come on, Teddy, this idea to buy cattle just isn't going to work this year. We were short of time as it was. Now, after all these delays, we'll never be able to get a herd bought and drive it home before winter," he argued. "I say we call it a day and skedaddle for home."

"We can't do that," I maintained. "Remember, the reverend told the sheriff where we are from. You can bet Sheriff Len will show up there looking for us one day."

"Well, what can we do?" Preacher Tom asked.

"I say we do what we started. We find them kids and get our stuff back. Then we go after Riley Hunt."

"Shoot, Teddy. I think getting knocked off your horse scrambled your brains," Bobby said. "How do you expect us to pull this off, with no guns and no horses?"

"I got a good idea where we can get some horses," I said, and glanced at Wiesmulluer. I cringed away from the explosion I knew would come when I outlined my plan. "Once we get our hands on some horses, we can slip into town and appropriate some guns."

"You mean steal them?" Bobby corrected.

"I mean borrow them," I countered. "You're always bragging about your experience. The job should be a piece of cake for you."

"What about the horses? Where are they?" Wiesmulluer asked, his voice hard with suspicion.

"Bertha's place," I answered and outlined the rest of my plan. Like I figured, Wiesmulluer balked, objecting to every part of the plan. I swear, he was still complaining the next morning when we stopped on the ridge overlooking Bertha's cabin.

"I ain't doing it. I ain't going down there," he declared, digging in his heels and getting all stubborn on us.

"You ain't scared of her, are you?" I asked, hoping to goad him into doing his part.

Wiesmulluer crossed his arms and looked away. ''That old battle-ax is crazy,'' he said and pouted.

''Karl! You shouldn't talk about Bertha that way. I'd say she is a fine, decent woman and quite attractive too,'' Preacher Tom said, a note of wistfulness in his voice at the end of his little speech.

''If you like her so much, then you go,'' Wiesmulluer grumbled.

''He can't. It's you that Bertha is sweet on,'' I said, patting Wiesmulluer's shoulder. I tried, but I couldn't keep a grin off my face and a feeling of satisfaction out of my voice. The way I saw it, Wiesmulluer deserved this for being so grouchy all the time. ''Look, all you have to do is keep her busy for a few minutes while we slip and get some horses.''

Wiesmulluer mumbled under his breath, digging a hole in the ground with the toe of his boot. ''All right,'' he conceded kicking a rock. ''But you better be quick about getting them horses. I don't want to be stuck in there with her all night.''

''Don't worry,'' Bobby said, giving him a cheerful grin. ''Just tell her a story and let her sit on your lap. We'll whistle at you when we're ready.''

I had to laugh as Wiesmulluer walked stiffly down to the cabin. ''Looks like a man going to his own hanging,'' I commented, then dove to the ground as the cabin door creaked open.

Hunkered down behind a rock, I watched as Bertha waddled out of the cabin, toting a huge basket of laundry. It seemed a strange time to be hanging out the wash, just a few minutes short of sundown, but then, I reckoned, Bertha was a strange woman.

She was halfway to the clothesline before she noticed Wiesmulluer. "Sugar!" she cried out gleefully and dropped the basket at her feet.

"A dollar says he loses his nerve and runs," Bobby whispered, but he got no takers.

For a second, it looked like Wiesmulluer would run. He froze dead in his tracks, his head whipping back and forth like a cornered rat. Yes, sir, he might have run, but Bertha never gave him the chance. She bounced over to him and grabbed his arm. To my amazement, she smacked a slobbery kiss on his weather-beaten cheek.

"That woman has definitely been living alone too long," Bobby said, shaking his head in wonderment.

"I reckon," I said, watching as Bertha drug the old man into the house. "Let's go get them horses."

Running crouched over, we scurried down the hill, diving into the barn as Wiesmulluer let out a yelp from inside the cabin. "What about saddles?" Bobby asked, laughing as we heard a crash from inside the cabin.

Ignoring Bobby's question, I looked around the dark barn. Something was wrong here. The place was stacked to the rafters with horses. Why, there must have been twenty horses in this barn. Squinting my eyes, I tried to see into the darkness and wondered if I dare strike a light.

"I found saddles. A bunch of them," Mr. Claude called.

As he spoke the horse closest to me jerked his head up. Now what the devil was that all about. Stepping in closer, I lit a match, shielding the flame from the door with my body. As the meager yellow light spread out in front of me, I swore, dropping the match.

"What are you trying to do, get us caught?" Bobby hissed, reaching around me with his toe to grind the match out.

"That was Mr. Claude's horse," I whispered.

Before we had a chance to check out the rest of the horses, we heard the sound of riders coming down the trail. As one we crept out the door, peering out at the trail.

"*Mon Dieu*! What are they doing here?" Claude exclaimed.

"How did they ever find us?" Bobby wondered.

"What does it matter now?" I said with a croak, my voice squeaky and my throat dry all of a sudden. "We are all dead men now!"

Chapter Seven

"We could just slip away. Let Wiesmulluer face the music," Bobby suggested, his eyes following the riders as they dipped into a gully and out of sight.

"Yeah! Let's go!" Mr. Claude agreed, tugging frantically at my sleeve.

"Are you crazy?" I asked, pulling away from Claude's grasp. "You can leave if you want to. Me, I wouldn't miss this for the world."

By then, I was moving, running low, trying to keep the house between me and the group of riders. Evidently, on second thought, the others wanted to see the show because I heard a scurry of movement behind me. We slid to a stop behind the house as the riders pounded into the yard. We could hear their voices as their horses milled about in front of the house.

We weren't so much interested in them riders as what was going on inside the house. Bunching our heads together, we crowded up to the small, fly-specked window. The scene inside that cabin had to be one of the weirdest I ever did see, or ever hope to. Wiesmulluer sat at the table, with Bertha sprawled in his lap. Snickering into my hand, I turned and looked at the others.

Bertha twirled a strand of his hair around her finger, looking at that old man like he was a honey-dipped biscuit. Giggling, she nuzzled his cheek.

Cringing away from her, Wiesmulluer looked like a man eating raw onions, but I can tell you, when that door crashed open his expression changed mighty fast. It went from sour to pure terror as his wife, Marie, walked in.

For a long second, time seemed to just stand still in that tiny shack. Wiesmulluer sat frozen, his mouth open. He looked like a man who just realized he squatted on a bear trap. The trap hadn't snapped shut, but he knew it was going to, and there wasn't a thing he could do about it.

Bertha looked angry at the interruption, but her anger was nothing compared to the fury stamped on Marie Wiesmulluer's face. "Karl Wiesmulluer!" she snapped, stamping her foot.

The sound of her voice seemed to whip old man Wiesmulluer out of his trance. 'Course, the anger in her voice could have woken the dead. I know it sure put a bee in his bonnet.

"Marie, darling," he cried, which shocked me—I never heard him use words like "darling."

Wiesmulluer tried to get up, but Bertha was too heavy. He fell back, the chair collapsing into splinters underneath them. They crashed to the floor with Bertha on top.

"Karl, what is the meaning of all this?" Marie asked, her words grinding out between clenched teeth. "What are you doing with this floozy?" she asked, looking like a hornet's nest that's been kicked over.

Wiesmulluer pushed Bertha off and scrambled to his feet. He slicked down his face and hurriedly wiped Bertha's red powder from his cheeks. "Look, dear, I can explain," he said, grinning sickly.

"Hey, you big lummox! Watch what you are doing," Bertha sputtered, her voice muffled by the dress up over her head. Rolling on the floor, she batted furiously at her dress. Once she finally got her dress pulled back down where it belonged, Bertha struggled to her feet.

Bertha glared at Wiesmulluer, her face even redder than usual. "I don't know who this tramp is," she said, pointing a finger at Marie Wiesmulluer. "But you better tell her to leave."

"Tramp!" Marie screamed, and threw down her purse. Now, I don't rightly know who Marie was going to tackle, and truthfully, I was laughing too hard to care.

Sheriff Len came through the door in a rush. He stepped into the center of the room, a bewildered look on his face. All of a sudden, my laughter stopped as Marie and Karl's two daughters, Betsy and Eddy, stepped into the tiny cabin.

"Oh, crud, we're in trouble now," Bobby whispered, but if he was talking to me, he was too late.

I took one look at Eddy's face and knew I best make myself scarce. Scurrying on my hands and knees, I made a beeline for the barn. The trip was a short one. I rounded the corner of the house and ran smack-dab into Weeb and Abner. Both of them wore deputy's stars and carried guns.

"Well, looky what we found, the welsher," Weeb said, and pointed his gun down at me. "How about it, boy? You got my money?"

"No," I replied meekly. "But I'm working on it."

"Well, you ain't working hard enough. Now, all of you on your feet. We'll see what the sheriff has to say about this," Weeb said decisively.

Our heads hanging, we trooped around to the front of the cabin and on inside. The place wasn't the bloodbath I expected. Somehow, Sheriff Len had taken control of the situation.

Old man Wiesmulluer was backed into the far corner, looking like a coon treed by a pack of dogs. Wanting to stick together, we rushed over to him and circled our wagons.

"Sheriff, what are you going to do with my husband?" Marie Wiesmulluer asked quietly.

Sheriff Len frowned and looked out the window. "I don't rightly know," he admitted after a lengthy pause. He walked over to the window. He wiped his finger over the windowsill and clucked his tongue as a mountain of dust cascaded to the floor. "Bertha, we are borrowing some of your horses. We'll take these men to town and straighten out this mess there. Weeb, you and Abner go saddle some horses."

"You can't do that! Those horses belong to me. You got no right to take them," Bertha objected.

"They ain't your horses! They're ours!" Claude exploded.

"What?" Sheriff Len asked, whirling around from the window.

"It's true," Claude maintained. "I saw my own horse in her barn. She knows the people who stole them!"

"He's lying, Sheriff. Don't listen to him. Those horses belong to me," Bertha said, and branded Louis with a darting glance.

Claude balled his fist, muttering in French as he took a step forward. Bertha wasn't at all intimidated. In fact, she stepped up to meet him.

"Settle down, both of you!" Sheriff Len snapped. He dropped into a chair, and rubbed his temples like a man with a powerful headache. ''I asked for this job,'' he muttered, looking down at the floor. ''I must have been crazy.''

To tell the truth, I felt sorry for the sheriff. I knew exactly what he was going through. I'd been there myself. Now, I felt sorry for him, but I wasn't about to do anything. Right now, no one was yelling at me, but I knew, if I opened my mouth that would change.

Sheriff Len raised his head, looking at Weeb and Abner. ''Go ahead. Saddle the horses, including one for Bertha. We'll sort all this out in town.''

As the two deputies turned to do his bidding, Sheriff Len took off his hat and tossed it on the table. Bertha crossed her arms, tapping her foot as she glowered at the sheriff. The next few minutes were a bit tense, with nobody speaking.

Weeb busted in through the door, making all of us jump. ''Sheriff, something's wrong here.''

''What are you talking about?'' Sheriff Len asked tiredly.

''In the barn, there's a stack of saddles yea high,'' he said, holding his hand at shoulder level. ''Well, we looked in the saddlebags and we found letters and stuff with their names on it.''

Sheriff Len swore, slamming his fist down on the table. ''Bertha! What in tarnation is going on here? How come you got all their stuff?''

''It ain't theirs; it's mine. I bought it fair and square.''

"Bought it? From who?"

Bertha shrugged, then placed her hand on her wide hips. "How should I know? I'm in the business of trading horses, not asking questions."

Sheriff Len swore again, shifting his glance to us. "You say you were going south to buy cattle and were robbed. Can you describe the men that robbed you?"

We all looked at one another, shifting our feet and hanging our heads. None of us wanted to own up to the fact that we had been robbed by a bunch of kids. "There was three of them. They ambushed us. We didn't get a good look at them," Mr. Claude finally said.

"Yeah, that's right," I agreed as the others nodded quickly, backing us up.

Sheriff Len looked at Marie Wiesmulluer and her daughters. "Is that the truth?"

"They left home to buy cattle," Marie answered, and glared at her husband. "Who knows what they have been up to since then. Karl, would you care to explain what is going on here?"

Clearly, Wiesmulluer didn't want to. "It was all Teddy's idea," he blustered and wormed in behind me.

"Teddy, you planned this?" Eddy asked.

"Well sorta," I admitted. "After we left town."

"After you broke jail, you mean," Sheriff Len corrected.

"Yeah, I guess. Anyway, after we left town, we figured to find the men who really robbed the bank. We found them and got the money, but then we were robbed and set afoot again," I explained.

Eddy gave me a sweet smile I didn't trust. I knew she was as temperamental as a store-bought stove. "That still doesn't explain how my father came to be in the arms of this woman."

"We needed horses. I knew Bertha had a barnful, so we decided to borrow some from her."

"Steal them you mean," Bertha said accusingly.

"Not exactly," I said, fudging the truth a mite. " 'Course, we didn't figure Bertha would agree to lend them, so we sent Karl in to distract her while we slipped the horses out of the barn. We meant to bring them back."

Eddy sighed and cut her eyes to the ceiling. "That was the best plan you could come up with?"

"Never mind that," Sheriff Len cut in excitedly. "You said you recovered the money. Where's it at?"

"It was took from us when we were robbed," Bobby admitted.

The sheriff swore under his breath. "How about the man that robbed the bank, who was he?"

"Riley Hunt."

"How did you find Hunt?" the sheriff asked quickly.

"Bobby knew of an outlaw hideout back in the canyons. We went there and Hunt was already there," I answered.

"A thieves' hideout," Sheriff Len repeated, scratching his chin. "We've been hearing about such a place for years, but I never believed the rumors. Now, you say the place exists. You've actually been there?"

"Sure, lots of times," Bobby replied with a shrug.

"Could you take me there?" the sheriff asked excitedly.

"Well, I don't know about that," Bobby said, tugging at his collar. "Taking a lawman out there would be a breach of ethics."

"Ethics?" Sheriff Len asked, disbelief ringing in his voice. "It's been said that you robbed the Overland Stage five times in one week. Shoot, I even heard you broke into the Governor's mansion and cleaned out his private safe."

Bobby laughed and waved a hand at the sheriff. "Aw, them's just fairy tales."

"Yeah, I bet," Sheriff Len said. "After all the things you are supposed to have done, it takes a lot of gall for you to even talk about ethics."

Bobby grinned, cocking his head. "Never knew I had them myself, but then I reckon nobody's perfect."

"You said you took the money from Riley Hunt," Sheriff Len pointed out, a sly look coming to his face.

"It seems to me that catching him might be in your best interest. I don't think Riley is the kind of feller to take something like that lying down. I reckon he's looking for you right now."

Sheriff Len had a point. We could all see that.

"All right," I said heavily. "We'll help you."

"Not you," Sheriff Len said, shaking his head firmly. "You are going to jail."

"Jail! What for?" I howled.

"You still owe Weeb twenty dollars. I told you, welshing on a bet is a crime in these parts."

"You were gambling again?" Eddy asked, her eyebrows shooting toward the sky.

I took a step back. I couldn't tell if she was mad, but I didn't figure to take any chances. "We needed the money," I explained sullenly.

Eddy smiled sadly, patting me on the chest. "So you lost twenty dollars you didn't have. Tell me, Teddy, did you come up with that idea all by yourself?"

"It seemed like a good plan at the time," I said, starting to get mad as she laughed. "We were in a jam."

"Well, I can see where gambling really helped you out," Eddy said, still laughing as I ground my teeth and looked at my friends for support, but all of a sudden, they all had dirt under their fingernails that needed attention.

Eddy turned to the sheriff. "If I paid Teddy's fine, would he still have to go to jail?"

"I suppose that would be all right," the sheriff decided. "As long as Weeb doesn't object.

Weeb scrunched up his eyebrows, and his big Adam's apple bounced up and down as he chewed his tobacco. "Now, I don't know," he said. That suited me fine. I wasn't at all sure I wanted Eddy paying my fine. If she did, I knew I would never hear the end of it.

Weeb scratched his chin and pulled at the seat of his britches. "Seems to me that a little time in the hoosegow might teach this young feller a lesson. It ain't right that this little lady should have to pay his truck."

Eddy stepped away from me, laying her hand on Weeb's shoulder. "It's okay, Mr. Weeb. Teddy and I are going to be married. I suppose I should get used to cleaning up his messes. Besides, he needs all the help he can get."

"Any fool can see that," Weeb said gruffly, his face turning red as Eddy smiled up at him. "Aw, all right, I guess it would be okay."

"Now, just one cotton-pickin' minute," I roared. I was mad as a mashed cat, but I wasn't quite sure why. "Maybe I don't want her paying. I can square my own debts."

A black look of anger swept across Weeb's face as he jabbed me in the gizzard with his rifle. "You jest shut your yap. If the young lady wants to pay what you owe, that ain't none of your concern. You just tell her thank you."

I was mad enough to eat nails, and the fact that Weeb kept jabbing me with that danged rifle didn't help any. I done made up my mind I wasn't going to allow this. 'Course, as usual, Eddy didn't leave me any choice. She just upped her nose at me, then paid Weeb the money.

He took the money, giving me a mighty scowl. "You best straighten up and treat this lady right. I'm gonna be keeping an eye on you."

"Now that we got that all settled, let's go get Riley Hunt," Sheriff Len said, champing at the bit.

Leaving Weeb to make sure the ladies got into town, we trooped out to the barn, where Abner was just finishing saddling the horses. Not only had he found our saddles, he found our guns and boots, stacked on a pile of feed.

"I still say you got no right to take that stuff," Bertha complained, standing in the door of the barn. "I paid good money for it."

"Bertha, if I was you, I'd keep quiet and hope that I forget that you have a barn full of stolen stuff," Sheriff Len warned, his tone icy. He swung aboard his horse, then looked down at Bertha. "We'll have a long talk about this when I get back."

He didn't scare Bertha; the red-faced woman just grunted and muttered a few choice comments at our backs as we rode out of the yard. We turned and waved at the women. Wiesmulluer swore under his breath. "How in the world did they end up here?" he wondered.

"That's my fault, I'm afraid," Sheriff Len confessed. "After I heard your story in the jail the other day, I decided to do some checking on you fellers. You story sounded like it might be true, so I sent a telegram."

"We don't have a telegraph station in Whiskey City," I pointed out.

"So I discovered, but they have one in Central City. Which I take it is near your town?" He looked at us and we nodded. "They knew of you there and vouched for your character. When your wife came to my office, she said she spoke to the stage driver from Central City, and he told her of your troubles. So they came to help." Sheriff Len turned to look back, but Bertha's cabin was already gone from sight. "I'm sorry if I got you boys in trouble, but I was just doing my job."

"You mean if we had stayed in jail, you would have set us free?" Preacher Tom asked, looking back at Bobby with a dark scowl.

"Yeah," Len said, with a small laugh. "After I got a reply on my telegraph, I was coming to turn you loose. That's when I found out you was gone."

"How did you know we would be at Bertha's?" I asked, scratching my head.

"I didn't. After your womenfolk showed up, they demanded that I help them find you. As you know, I'm sure they can be most persuasive. We only stopped at Bertha's to water our horses. We had no idea you'd be there."

We rode a long ways in silence. Then the sheriff spoke again. "Tell me about the men that robbed you."

We never got a chance to answer. The sheriff had said that Riley would be hunting us, and we believed it, but still we had been careless. We didn't even know Riley Hunt and his men were near until they opened up on us.

The first wave of bullets swept Sheriff Len from the saddle like a giant flyswatter. He flipped backward out of the saddle and rolled over the back end of his horse.

Chapter Eight

Even as Sheriff Len crashed to the ground, I dove off my horse, taking my rifle with me. Clutching my rifle, I looked for a place to hide. A small trench cut by runoff water during the last rain ran a few feet to our left. That little ditch wasn't much, but it was all the cover to be had.

Pointing at the ditch with my rifle, I hollered at the others. Using our milling horses as cover, we scurried for the ditch. Bobby and Claude had the sheriff, dragging him into the scant cover of the trench.

As I flopped into the ditch, I heard a cry. Looking over the rim of the ditch, I saw Preacher Tom on the ground, holding a bloody shoulder. Without thinking, I dropped my rifle and dove out of the ditch on my belly. Stretching out as far as I could, I latched onto

Tom's ankle. With a mighty heave, I drug him over to the hole. Grabbing his belt, I flopped him over the edge as a hailstorm of bullets struck the place he'd just been.

That's when it struck me. Playtime was over. Riley Hunt wasn't messing around; he wanted us dead. His men were shooting to kill.

An anger boiled up in me as I stuck my rifle over the edge, firing as fast as I could work the action and pull the trigger. As I fired, I called them every name I could think of. And believe me, I've worked around Wiesmulluer long enough to get a right good education on the subject. The metallic click of a dry rifle finally registered in my brain, and I ducked back into the ditch.

"That ought to keep their heads down a minute. Come on. Let's move," Bobby said, tugging on my sleeve.

Dragging the wounded men with us, we scampered down the ditch thirty yards where it deepened and widened. There the ditch was five feet deep, giving us good protection. Abner found a spot and began returning fire, keeping them busy.

Mr. Claude stretched the sheriff out in the bottom of the ditch, making the lawman as comfortable as possible. "How bad is he hurt?" I asked, looking over his shoulder as Mr. Claude opened the sheriff's shirt.

"I'm not a doctor, but it looks mighty bad to me," he said, without even looking up. "He's bleeding awful bad. I'd say we best get him to a doctor and do it quick.''

''That may be a whole lot easier said than done,'' I said, but I knew Claude was right. Sheriff Len had two bullets in his chest and they both looked mighty serious.

''Teddy's right,'' Bobby said, his head above the rim of the ditch. He scanned the ground quickly, then slid back down beside me. ''This little draw plays out aways down the line. Face it, we're trapped!''

''You're just full of good cheer,'' Wiesmulluer observed as he slapped a rough bandage on Preacher Tom's wounded shoulder. ''You got any good news?''

''Well, Riley can't get down at us,'' Bobby replied.

''So it's a standoff?'' I asked; Bobby shrugged, then nodded his head.

''That ain't gonna work, boys,'' Claude said as he worked to stop the sheriff's bleeding. ''This man ain't got a lot of time.'' He stopped his work, looking at us and clenching his fist in anger. ''I'm doing all I can, but I don't know much about this kind of work. He needs a real doctor. We don't get him to a doctor, he's going to die.''

Nobody had anything to say to that. All we could do was huddle in our hole and wait. I took a peek over the lip of the ditch and saw what Bobby said was true. Between us and Hunt lay a hundred yards of open ground. The same behind us. We couldn't cross it and neither could they. On both sides, the canyon walls rose straight up. I suppose a man might climb them, but not before Hunt's men cut him to pieces.

As the afternoon wore on, it settled into a waiting game. A shot would occasionally split the stillness, but for the most part it was silent as a tomb.

Tomb. I shivered as the word came to mind. As a matter of fact, this ditch reminded me of a grave. I tried to push such morbid thoughts from my mind, not wanting to bring death down on us by thinking of it.

As I sat in the ditch, a plan began to take shape in my mind. It was crazy, even desperate, but right now, we were desperate and getting more so by the minute.

Crouching low, I crept down the trench to where Bobby sat, perched halfway up the side of the ditch. He saw me coming and slid down to the bottom. "We gotta do something. We have to get out of here," I said, trying to sound calm.

"I'm ready," Bobby said, pulling out his shirttail and wiping dust from his rifle. "You got any ideas? I've been thinking all day and I sure don't have any."

I pointed back behind us. "There's a bend in the canyon. Once a man got around the bend, he'd be out of sight."

"Sure, but what then? It's a long ways to go get help," Bobby pointed out.

"Maybe he could circle around and flank them. Maybe flush them out."

"I don't know, Teddy. That's a long run to get around the bend. I figure our best bet would be to wait until dark, then try to slip away."

"Carrying two wounded men? They'd hear us for sure. I figure dark is what they are waiting for. They could slip down on us easy in the dark," I argued.

His face stone serious, Bobby glanced at Sheriff Len. "You're right about that." He sat his rifle down and climbed up the back bank, studying the layout for a long time. "Okay, if a man was lucky, he might make it, but I doubt it."

"You guys can shoot and give me some cover. If you can keep their heads down, I ought to make it," I said, trying to sound more confident than I felt.

"Hey, who said anything about you going? You're slow as a gimpy turtle. Reckon I ought to be the one to go," Bobby said, giving me a cheerful grin.

He was right about that, but for some reason, I wanted to be the one to go. This was my fool plan, and I figured if anybody got killed trying it, it should be me. "We could both go," I suggested.

"That would mean one less gun keeping their heads down," Bobby pointed out.

"Yeah, but it would also give them one more target. It might give one of us a better chance."

Bobby smiled and pulled his pistol, checking the loads. "Aw, what does it matter? We'll both likely get killed, but then nobody lives forever."

I moved down the ditch, calling the others down to me. They looked at me and Bobby with shock as I outlined our plan. "Are you loco? There ain't a chance in a million of making that run," Wiesmulluer pointed out.

"Anybody got any better ideas?" I asked, but nobody did. "I figure if you guys pour it to them, you can keep them busy long enough to give us a good head start."

"And after that?" Claude asked.

Bobby grinned, patting the little Frenchman on the back. "After that, we figure to run like the devil hisself was chasing us."

"It'd take a good twenty seconds to make that run," Wiesmulluer said, rubbing his jaw. "That's a long time with men shooting at you."

"You got any better ideas?" I asked, and believe me, I was hoping he had something up his sleeve. He didn't. For once, that old man didn't have a thing to say. "If we're going, we best get at it," I said, wanting to go before I changed my mind and chickened out.

Abner took off his hat and wiped the sweat from his forehead, then spat. "I don't reckon you boys got a chance, but I want to wish you luck." He twisted his hat in his hands, then suddenly stuck out his hand awkwardly. "I'd like to shake your hands and wish you the best."

We pumped his hands, then Mr. Claude stepped up, shaking our hands and giving us a squeeze on the shoulder. Wiesmulluer started to say something. He wrung his hands, then swallowed hard. He looked down the ditch, unable to look either of us in the eye.

"Whatever you got on your mind, save it and tell us when we get back," Bobby told him.

"You boys take care," he said, then spun around and took his position.

"I'll say a prayer for you," Preacher Tom called weakly from where he lay.

"Thanks, we're going to need all the help we can get," I said softly, then looked at Bobby. "Last one there stands for drinks tonight."

"You're on," Bobby said, and somehow he managed a grin, but I noticed a slight quiver in his hands as he picked up his rifle. Well, he wasn't alone, for I was shaking inside myself.

"You ready?" I asked, and he nodded. "All right, on the count of three," I said and started counting.

Chapter Nine

When I reached three, we scrambled out of the ditch and took off running. We ran bent over, clutching our rifles. While I ran a zigzag course, trying to make myself a harder target, Bobby ran hard in a straight line. I reckon he figured the shortest distance is a straight line, and he wanted to get there as quick as he could.

I didn't bother to look back, but it sounded like a war had broken out behind us. I felt a surge of pride well up inside me. Our friends were doing all they could to give us cover. They were firing more than I would have dreamed possible. Hunt's men must feel like they had been caught in a hailstorm, I thought, feeling a wave of savage satisfaction. Only a few shots came our way, and none of them hit very close to us.

Bobby beat me around the bend by a good twenty yards. By the time I reached him, he was bent over at the waist, laughing between gasps. "We made it!" he said, his voice shaky as a store-bought chair.

Well, he wasn't the only one shaking; my legs were knocking like a threshing machine. "I told you we would," I said, grinning from ear to ear.

"That you did," Bobby boomed, putting his arm around my shoulder. "I never doubted you for a second. It was a great plan, and by the way, you owe me a drink."

I did at that, and I also owed Wiesmulluer, Claude, and Abner a drink. Maybe more than one. They saved our bacon, shooting the way they did.

"Boy, them fellers done some shootin'. Sounded like an army blasting away back there," Bobby said, almost reading my mind.

We found a likely place to climb out of the canyon. Loosening my belt a notch, I shoved my rifle down in it to keep my hands free. Using our hands and toes, we worked our way up to the top.

As our heads cleared the lip of the canyon, a cool breeze greeted us, drying the sweat we'd worked up during the climb. Standing up, I looked across the country. I never did see a place so cut by canyons and washes.

"Kinda purty, ain't it?" Bobby said, standing beside me.

"It sure is," I agreed. The place had a wild, free beauty. I could look at it all day, but we weren't here to see the sights.

After a quick check of our rifles, we took off, moving along at a trot. We moved fast, but we still kept a wary eye out for trouble. Stumbling into one ambush was enough to suit us for one day. We figured that Riley knew what we were up to and might send some men to slow us down.

We encountered no such difficulties. By the time we worked into position to attack, Riley Hunt and his men were long gone. We could see their dust cloud a good two miles away and moving fast.

"We must be mighty fierce men, indeed, to put such a scare into them. Look at them go," Bobby chortled as he watched the dust cloud grow smaller.

He wouldn't have been so happy if he'd been looking at what I was. I was looking down at our friends and could plainly see that they were no longer alone. Unable to tear my eyes away, I reached out, flailing my arm a couple of times until I found Bobby's shoulder. "Never mind that! Look," I said, pointing down at our friends. Now we knew how they'd been able to fire so much; they'd had help.

Bobby turned to look, then abruptly sat down on a rock. He took off his hat, studying it intently as he wiped the sweat from the bank. "This is like a nightmare. It just keeps getting worse and worse," he mumbled to himself.

I closed my eyes and sighed. "Well, we might as well go face the music and get it over with," I said heavily.

"Yeah," Bobby said, a sense of dread in his voice. He stood up slowly, clapping his hat back on his head. "Let's get it over with."

Feeling old as the hills, we retraced our steps. While we stumbled along, I tried to figure out what I'd ever done to deserve this. I mean, I knew I was no angel. I'd wandered off the straight and narrow a time or two, but never in my life had I done anything really bad. You know, like stealing horses or cheatin' at poker. No, sir, nothing nowhere near bad enough to deserve this.

By the time we reached our friends, they were fixing a litter for Sheriff Len. Weeb sat on an ugly gray stallion, a rifle across the saddle. "Looked like we showed up in time," he said, grinning down at us.

"How did you get here?" I asked.

"We rode," Weeb answered, laughing heartily. "We was just fixin' to leave Bertha's when we heard the shots. I figured you might need some help so I hustled over here." Weeb leaned over the saddle and spat. Chuckling to himself, he wiped his hand on the back of his glove. "I tried to leave the women behind, but they would have none of it. I didn't see any way short of shooting them to stop them, so here we are."

I glanced at Eddy, but she was completely ignoring me. "Are you going to help or stand there blabbing all day?'' Marie Wiesmulluer asked as she wound a long bandage around Sheriff Len's chest.

You can believe we pitched in and helped. We were in the doghouse and were willing to do anything to get out. We hustled down the canyon where Wiesmulluer and Claude were rounding up our horses.

As we snared the last two, Wiesmulluer looked off in the direction Riley Hunt and his men took. ''You know,'' he said, a crafty look in his old eyes, ''we got those outlaws on the run. If we took after them now, we might catch them flatfooted. I figure between the ladies and Weeb and Abner, they got things well in hand here.''

Now I figured he musta cracked his head when he dove off his horse. We'd been walking and riding, mostly walking for days, and he still hadn't got his fill. ''You want to chase after them now? I was looking forward to a hot meal and sleeping in a soft bed tonight.''

''Are you crazy?'' Mr. Claude whispered, shushing me. ''The last thing we want to do is go into town.''

''Why not?'' Bobby asked, looking at me and rolling his eyes.

''When you boys have been married as long as Karl and I, you'll learn, there's times you want to keep away from your wife. Right now, them women are still mad. Give them a chance to cool down, then apologize,'' Mr. Claude said in a fatherly tone.

"What you mean is, if we lay low for a while, they'll forget this whole thing ever happened?" Bobby asked, sounding mighty pleased.

"Are you kidding?" Wiesmulluer said with a snort as the smile drained off Bobby's face. Wiesmulluer shook his head. "They ain't never gonna forget this. Every time you screw up, you're going to hear about this."

That was a sobering idea, especially for me, as I'm prone to screw things up. "Let's go tell them we're going after Hunt," I suggested, that soft bed no longer so appealing.

Well, we pitched the idea, but it got squashed like a stinkbug. I reckon the women had a bone to pick with us, and they didn't want us riding away and maybe getting ourselves killed before they got in their shots.

We didn't argue much, trying to keep things friendly but knowing that wouldn't last. You could see, those women were mad. Even so, we hoped for the best as we loaded Sheriff Len on the litter. Preacher Tom claimed he could ride, so we boosted him into the saddle and headed for town.

We rode out in a tight group, but that didn't last. Very quickly, the group began to split into pairs. Bertha rode beside Preacher Tom, practically fawning over him. For a man with a bullet in his shoulder, the reverend looked awfully happy.

Weeb and Abner rode beside the sheriff, trying to give the lawman all the comfort they could. He was conscious and had to be in pain, but he rode in tight-lipped silence.

Tight-lipped silence—that pretty much summed up the way Wiesmulluer rode. Marie had him pulled off to one side, and while I couldn't hear her words, I could tell she was really giving him the business. The way she shook her finger in his face, I figured she was gonna put an eye out.

I can tell you, however, there was nothing silent about Mr. Claude and his wife. Waving their arms frantically, they screeched and caterwauled at each other like a flock of magpies. The only trouble was, they were jabbering in French, and I couldn't understand a blamed thing they said.

Me and Bobby grinned at each other, truly enjoying the older men's discomfort. Little did we know, the same fate waited on us.

I kept looking back where Betsy and Eddy rode side by side. My heart ached to talk to Eddy. I missed her something terrible. But I figured Mr. Claude's advice was good. I could tell she wasn't happy with me, and I best lie low till she cooled down. If she wanted to give me the silent treatment, I'd take it and just be glad that she wasn't raking my backside. Still, I yearned to talk to her, if only just for a second. 'Course, there is that old saying: Be careful what you wish for, 'cause you just might get it.

Pretty soon, Eddy rode up beside us. "Bobby, would you excuse us? I want to have a word with Teddy. Besides, Betsy has something to say to you."

I groaned inside and glanced quickly at Bobby, who looked like a man about to be taken out and shot. Them girls hadn't been giving us the silent treatment, they'd been planning their method of attack.

As Bobby dropped back, I looked at Eddy and a thrill rushed through me. That didn't last long. "Theodore Cooper, have you lost your mind?" Eddy asked, not wasting any time.

"I don't think so," I said warily.

"I wonder," she said quietly. "I'm not even going to mention all that nonsense about my father and Bertha." I snorted, knowing full well that she was going to mention it aplenty, and I was right. "They said that whole mess was your idea. You should be ashamed of yourself. Bertha is a nice woman."

"She had our horses! I wouldn't be a bit surprised if she wasn't in cahoots with the . . . ah . . . the people who stole them from us," I declared.

"Oh, pooh. Don't be ridiculous," Eddy scoffed. "And keep your voice down, she might hear you," Eddy warned, glancing quickly at Bertha. But Bertha wasn't paying any attention to anything but the reverend. Eddy turned back to me. "All of that isn't the problem. It's the other stuff you did."

Now that was a head scratcher. If she wasn't mad about that, what in the world could she be mad about?

I stole a glance at her face. Maybe she wasn't mad at all. Her black eyes weren't popping and snapping like they usually did when she was really peeved.

To my surprise, she reached over and took my hand. "Teddy, I'm worried about you. What has gotten into you? You broke out of jail. You stole some horses in town and took what you needed from the store. Then, to top things off, when we found you, you were calmly setting about to steal some horses from Bertha."

"Those were our horses!" I objected, but she only snorted and rolled her eyes. "Anyway, we didn't exactly steal that stuff from the store in town. I left a note, and I'll go back and pay for that stuff."

Eddy frowned and tucked a stray strand of black hair behind her ear. "Don't bother. Mother already took care of that," she said curtly. Then to my surprise, she smiled and even laughed a little. "Teddy, I swear, you're like a pig in a parlor sometimes. I know you mean well, but it wouldn't hurt to stop and use your head sometimes."

"Yeah, I reckon you're right about that," I admitted. "But sometimes you get in a jam and you have to wade in swinging with both fists."

She patted my hand, giving me a superior look. "You see, there's your problem. If you would just think about it long enough, there's always a way out without resorting to fighting. If you would have taken a moment and used your head, you would have realized that you were innocent and there was no need to break out of jail. In fact, the sheriff was going to turn you loose.''

''I know,'' I said miserably, ''but Bobby wanted to get out of jail. He said the only way to prove our innocence was to catch the real thieves.''

Eddy leaned in close, darting a glance back at Bobby and Betsy. ''Well, I guess it isn't all your fault. I know you listen to Bobby and he gets you into trouble. Now, don't get me wrong; I like Bobby, but he's wild and reckless. You need to take some time and think before he talks you into doing these things.''

Bobby was my partner, and I really liked him, but if shifting some of the blame over to him was going to get me off the hook, I was gonna do it. I figured the man that said all is fair in love and war knew what he spoke of.

''I promise, I won't listen to him so much from now on.''

''Good,'' she said, and smiled delightfully.

Weeb steered his horse over beside us, a smile on his blocky face. ''Boy, I reckon I owe you an apology,'' he said, and whacked me on the back with enough force to floor a buffalo. ''I had you pegged for a good-for-nothing whiner, but I reckon I was wrong. I saw what you and that other young feller done today, and that took guts. You boys is fighters! I admire that.''

"Thanks," I said, shifting uncomfortably in the saddle. "If you hadn't come along and pitched in, we probably wouldn't have made it."

Weeb laughed and waved off my thanks as if it were of no consequence. "Likely that's right, but you mighta made it on your own," he said, but there was doubt in his voice. He looked at Eddy, his face rock serious as he scratched the stubble on his chin. "You got a good man there, missy. If I was you, I'd hang onto him."

"Thank you, sir. I intend to."

Weeb shifted in the saddle, his eyes boring into me. "And you, young feller, this little filly helped to save your bacon. Have you thanked her right and proper?"

"No. I was just getting around to that," I said, none too happy with Weeb. I figured, I'd hear about how she pulled my fat out of the fire enough, without him bringing it up.

Maybe Weeb knew I was mad at him or maybe he just said all he had to say, but either way, he pulled his horse away, giving us room to talk.

We didn't talk, though. Not for a long while. "Eddy, Weeb was right. If you hadn't showed up when you did, them boys mighta salted us away." I took off my hat, twisting it in my hand as I looked at the setting sun. "What I'm trying to say is . . . thanks." Eddy started to say something, but I held up my hand. There was some things I had to say, and I was gonna do it. "About all that other stuff, I'm plumb sorry. You was right, I didn't think, but I was missing you so bad, I couldn't think straight.''

Now, I suppose, every once in a while even a clod like me has to stumble around and say the right thing, and boy, I sure did it this time. Eddy threw her arms around my neck and gave me a kiss. She almost knocked me out of the saddle, but the way I was feeling right then, I reckon I woulda floated to the ground. I know, the ride the rest of the way into town was sure more enjoyable.

It was late and very dark when we rode slowly into Miles City. Weeb led us down the deserted streets to the doctor's house. Evidently, the doctor heard us or he was watching out the window because he rushed out of the house to meet us. He was barefoot and wore no hat as he carried the lantern down the walk.

One thing you had to say for the doctor, he never wasted any time asking fool questions. ''Hold this,'' he said, handing the lantern to Claude. The doctor bent over the sheriff, then reached back and grabbed Claude's arm. ''Get that light over here where I can see something,'' he growled. He looked at Sheriff Len's wounds, then jabbed a finger at me and Wiesmulluer. ''You two, get this man inside.''

Dragging Claude with him, the doc moved over to Preacher Tom. He shoved Bertha aside, then pulled back the reverend's shirt. ''Who bandaged this?'' he bellowed.

''I did,'' Marie said, her voice small as a mouse's.

"Good job," the doc said with a grunt and began removing the bandages.

"Is he going to be all right? Bertha asked breathlessly.

"Bertha, I can't examine this man with you breathing down my neck. Give me some room." He made a clucking sound as he looked Tom over. "You can wait," he said.

He looked to where me and Wiesmulluer was just lifting the sheriff off the litter. "I thought I told you to get that man inside. What is he still doing out here?"

Grumbling under our breath and shooting mean looks at the doc, we carried Sheriff Len inside the house. We started to lay him on a sofa, but the doctor threw a fit. "Not there. Carry him in here," he commanded, holding back a curtain that divided the room. "Put him on that cot," he said, then jabbed a finger at Preacher Tom. "You, set in that chair. I'll get to you once I finish the sheriff," he told Tom. "The rest of you get out," he added, rolling up his sleeves.

"Do you need any help, doctor? I would be glad to stay and help you," Eddy offered.

The doc looked at her over the top of his spectacles. "Are you a doctor?"

"No, but I could . . ."

"Then you wouldn't be much help, would you? You'd just be under foot asking all kinds of fool questions. I don't need that. Now run along."

In a tight bunch we trooped outside. We stopped at the doctor's gate. "I'll go take care of the horses," I said, volunteering.

"I'll help you," Eddy said, shooting a scorching look at the doctor. "Maybe I can do that without being in the way."

If she expected to get under the doctor's skin, she was in for a disappointment. He just looked up and frowned. "Are you people still here? Get out so I can go to work."

"Somebody ought to pop him in the mouth," Eddy grumbled as we shuffled out of his house.

I started to remind her of her own words that fighting never solved anything, but I wisely held my tongue. The mood she was in, she'd likely haul off and wallop me.

As the others shuffled down to the hotel, Eddy and I gathered the horses and led them to the livery. The place was deserted and dark, and we worked in silence. I didn't mind the silence, I enjoyed being close to her.

After we finished, we walked to the door, looking up at the sky. Tonight, the stars shone bright and clear, looking like bits of light someone had flung across the sky.

"I sure have missed you," I said, my voice low and husky.

We stepped close, our lips parting as our heads came together. All of a sudden, something cold and hard that felt a bunch like a gun barrel was jabbed roughly into my back. I staggered forward, banging my head into Eddy's.

Chapter Ten

"Hey! Watch it!" Eddy said, rubbing her forehead.

"Stuff the chatter in a feed bag," Stevie Hunt barked, and stepped around me where he could cover us both with his gun.

"Oh, Teddy, look. A boy out playing outlaw," she cried, her hands going to her mouth. "Isn't that sweet?"

"Hey lady, I ain't messing around! Now stick up your hands and give me all your money," Stevie ordered.

"Isn't he just precious," Eddy cooed.

"Eddy." I hissed a warning. Of course she wasn't paying any attention. She might think Junior there was a lovable little waif, but I knew better.

"Are you going to shoot us, little boy?" she asked, laughing as she patted him on top of the head.

Stevie slapped her hand away and jabbed her in the pit of the stomach with the pistol. "Give me all your money."

"Ow! Watch where you're pokin' that thing," Eddy shouted and ripped the gun from his hand.

I mean she did it that quick too. I hardly even seen it. I know Junior never expected it or even hardly knew when it happened.

"This is a real gun!" Eddy exclaimed. She handed the gun to me, slapping it against my chest. She bent down and shook her finger in his face. "Where did you get this gun? Do your folks know you are playing with it? You're too young to have a gun."

"Am not! Now give me that back," Stevie yelled. He tried to kick her in the shins, but I grabbed him first.

I jerked him clean off the ground and shook him a mite. "All right, Junior. Where's our money?" I growled fiercely.

"We hid it, and you ain't never gonna find it," he sputtered defiantly.

Eddy looked at me, confusion showing in her dark eyes. "Your money? Teddy, what is he talking about?" Slowly the confused look melted off her face, replaced by an amused look of understanding. "This little boy is one of the desperadoes who robbed you?" she asked, then laughed right in my face.

''They jumped us outta nowhere,'' I said, still holding the little brat off the ground. ''Anyway, there was three of them.''

''Oh, well, that makes all the difference.'' Now, if she was trying to keep a straight face, she sure wasn't doing a very good job at it. ''Tell me, were the other two as fearsome as this one?''

''They're trickier than they look,'' I informed her, then turned my attention back to the kid. ''If you know what's good for you, you'll tell me where the money is. It wouldn't take much for me to flog the tar outta you.''

''Teddy!'' Eddy snapped, stamping her foot on the ground. ''You're not going to lay a hand on that boy. Now quit acting like an ogre and put him down.''

I didn't want to do it, especially after the kid shot me a smirk of satisfaction. No, sir, I didn't want to do it, but I plopped him down on the ground, not bothering to be especially gentle. He jerked away from me, then straightened his shirt. ''How about giving my gun back now?''

''You won't be needing it, so I'll just hang onto it for a while,'' I said and made a face at the little brat.

''That's stealing!'' he said petulantly.

''You'll get over it,'' I assured him. ''Now we are going to the hotel.'' He crossed his arms, threatening to get all stubborn on me. Well, by now, I'd run smooth out of patience with young Stevie. With both hands I grabbed his shoulders and spun him around. "March!" I ordered and gave him a healthy shove.

"Teddy, be careful. He's just a little boy. You don't want to hurt him," Eddy cautioned, worrying like a mother hen over the boy.

"Don't waste your time worrying about him. He deserves whatever he gets. You can believe me on that," I said, taking her hand in mine as we followed along behind Junior. Once, he tried to make a break for it, but I snagged him by the collar and hauled him back.

"The hotel's thataway," I told him, then thumped him in the back of the head with my finger when he cussed at me.

"That's certainly not very nice language, Stevie. Where did you learn such words?" Eddy asked.

Junior looked back over his shoulder and gave me a wicked grin. "From him," he said, pointing his little finger at me. "That's nothing compared to what him and his friends said when me and my sisters tied them up."

"Sisters?" Eddy asked, looking at me out of the corner of her eye. I saw the look but pretended real hard like I never. "Teddy, you mean you guys, five grown men, were robbed by this young man and his two sisters?"

Well, I reckon them was the facts, but they sure sounded worse the way she laid them out. I didn't really have an answer that suited me so I kept my trap closed. I sure was glad when we reached the hotel.

We found our friends standing in the lobby, waiting while a yawning clerk checked them in. The clerk wore a nightshirt tucked into his britches and a soft pointy hat on his head, so I figured they must have roused him out of his bed.

Old man Wiesmulluer liked to have come out of his socks when he spotted Stevie Hunt. The color drained out of his face, and his lower lip quivered like a snake's tail. "You!" he sputtered, spitting all over Claude. Ol' Wiesmulluer's jaw sawed back and forth and he looked like he was going to explode, but I reckon he couldn't think of the right words. "You!" he roared again.

Now, it shames me to say that I took pleasure in the way Junior shied back from that old man. Not that I blamed him. Right then, Wiesmulluer was raging back and forth and frothing at the mouth like a rabid skunk. I reckon he coulda scared a bear outta his hole.

A whimper coming out of his mouth, Stevie shrank back against Eddy, clutching at her skirt.

Eddy put her arm around his pointy little head and glared at her father. "Daddy, you're scaring this poor young boy!"

"Poor young boy, my aching backside," Wiesmulluer snorted. "And believe me, I'm going to do more than scare him if he doesn't tell me where my money is!" Wiesmulluer thundered.

Little Stevie threw his arms around Eddy's waist. Sniffling, he looked up at her with wide eyes. ''Please, don't let them hurt me,'' he begged.

Now, I didn't buy all that sniffling and crying, not for one second. I reckon none of the men did, but Eddy sure went for it. She bought the bit lock, stock, and barrel. So did the other women. They flocked to Stevie like kids to a candy barrel. They hovered over him, patting his hair and wiping his nose.

''Would you just look at that,'' Bobby said disgustedly. ''That little prairie leech robbed us of all our money, and they're treating him like he was next in line to be king.''

''What that boy needs is a visit behind the woodshed,'' Mr. Claude said, his accent thick and heavy tonight.

''You'll have to wait in line. I get first whack at him,'' Wiesmulluer said. He smacked his fist into his palm and licked his lips. ''When I get done with him, he'll be old and gray before he can sit down.''

I heard Eddy ask the little brat why he took to robbing and stealing. I leaned in close, I wanted to hear the answer to that one myself.

Junior sniffled a couple of times and ran his finger back and forth under his nose. ''Well, after Ma died, we was all alone. We never knew where our pa was.'' He looked up at the women, his eyes wide as pie plates and mournful as a hound dog's. ''After a few days, the food ran out and we got real hungry. I never been so hungry in all my born days.'' He stopped and received a round of pats on the head along with a host of ''oh dears'' and ''little darlings.''

Looking pleased with himself, Stevie went on with his fairy tale. ''It'd been days since we ate, and we couldn't take it anymore so we snuck down to this ranch and stole some food. We knew stealing was wrong, but we was so hungry. After that, we tried our best to get what we needed honestly, but it wasn't easy. Sometimes we had to take things just to get by.'' Stevie hung his head, scuffing his toe against the floor. ''I reckon we knew it was wrong, but we had to eat.''

All of a sudden, he threw himself against Eddy, his sobs muffled by her dress. ''There, there.'' She comforted him and stroked his hair. ''Everything is going to be all right.''

He stepped back, rubbing his eyes. I looked close to see if he was crying or faking. His eyes were red, but I still figured he was faking. I mean, of course, his eyes were red, after the way he knuckled them. It was a wonder he hadn't pushed them out the back of his head.

Eddy knelt down in front of him and caressed his cheek with the back of her hand. ''Now, Stevie, this is very important. Can you tell us where your sisters are at?''

''Well, not exactly,'' he said huskily.

''Could you take Teddy there?'' she asked, and I groaned. My body was plumb tuckered. I sure didn't feel up to traipsing around the country all night.

Wiesmulluer stepped forward, glaring down at the boy. ''Is our money there?''

''No. We hid the money back in the hills.''

Wiesmulluer lost interest from there. He took his key from the clerk and tromped upstairs.

How far is it to where your sisters are camped?'' I asked tiredly. I just wanted to get this over with and get to bed.

Stevie shrugged. ''Not too far. Two, maybe three miles.''

Bobby stepped up, clapping me on the back. ''I'll go with you, Teddy boy. Make sure you don't get into trouble.''

Our horses sure didn't seem to like the idea of going back out so soon. They fought the bit and humped their backs, shying away as we saddled them. Well, if they weren't happy, they weren't alone. I wondered if I would ever sleep again. Yawning mightily, I took the lead rope for the spare horse and swung into my saddle.

Stevie led the way as we rode slowly out of town, the clopping of our horses' hooves sounding loud in the stillness of the night.

"How did things go between you and Eddy?" Bobby asked, hooking his leg over the saddlehorn and fixing himself a smoke.

I shrugged, fighting another yawn. "Not too bad," I replied, wondering if I should tell him what Eddy said. "Eddy figures that most of what happened was your fault. She figured you talked me into it. Claimed I shouldn't listen to you so much."

I stole a look over at him, but Bobby didn't look mad. As a matter of fact, he busted out laughing, his cigarette falling from his mouth. He had to scramble to keep it from burning his lap. Once he had the cigarette safely in his mouth again, he chuckled again. "You know, that's pretty much what Betsy told me. She said you don't think before you act and that I shouldn't follow you." We looked at each other and laughed. "So I want you to be sure and think extra hard tonight. Keep me out of trouble. I'm too tired for any more fighting and chasin' around," Bobby said, still chortling.

True to his word, Stevie led us to a place a couple of miles from town. "There's a cave up there. That's where they are at," he said and pointed to a nest of boulders.

Now, I had a real clear memory of what happened the last time he showed me his camp, so I figured to be extra careful tonight. After all, I didn't want to get Bobby in any trouble. I swung down, moving with care. I was watching the ground for booby traps, when I shoulda been watching in front of me.

The only warning I got was a slight whooshing sound. I heard that sound and my backside puckered, then bright lights exploded in my head.

Chapter Eleven

The lights exploding in my head, I fell to my knees. In a fog, I heard a scream and sensed a scurry of movement around me. Through eyes which were frosted up like a windowpane in December, I saw the club coming at my head another time. For a second, time seemed to freeze as that club whizzed at my head. My mind screamed for me to duck, but my muscles refused to respond.

That stick shattered over the top of my head. A shock ripped through my body that even made my toes tingle. My world a fuzzy, gray mist, I could hear voices screaming but couldn't make out what they said. My head buzzed like a beehive as I surged to my feet and pulled my gun.

Somebody grabbed me from behind, pinning my arms to my side. It was Bobby; I could hear his voice screaming in my ear. The fog in my eyes began to clear and I could see a blurry Joan Hunt standing in front of me. She held the broken club in both hands. Her little sister clung to her leg and a disheveled Stevie lay on the ground beside her. Suddenly, as if she just realized she was holding the thing, Joan screamed and flung the club to the ground.

"Are you all right, buddy?" Bobby asked. He loosened his grip on me, but didn't let go completely.

"What happened?" I mumbled.

"The young lady whacked you over the head—twice," Bobby said. He laughed a little under his breath. "Are you all right?" he asked and I nodded.

He let go of me, and I staggered forward and fell to my knees. From my knees, I shook my head several times to clear the cobwebs, but it didn't work very well.

"Are you sure you're not hurt? I'm so sorry that I hit you," Joan Hunt said, kneeling in front of me. She reached out hesitantly and started to touch my head, then pulled back. "I didn't mean to hit you, but when I heard someone coming, I was so scared. I didn't know what to do. Does it hurt much?"

I started to snap at her and tell her it didn't feel like a Sunday picnic, but she looked so shy and innocent. I couldn't bring myself to hurt her. "Aw, my head's awful hard. I reckon that stick got the worst of it."

I struggled to get to my feet. Joan grabbed my arm, helping me up. The world swam in front of my eyes, and if Joan hadn't been holding my arm, I reckon I woulda went timber again.

"Are we going to go to jail?" she asked.

"I don't rightly know," I said, my tongue feeling like my mouth was packed with cold syrup.

"If you told where the money is, Sheriff Len might not send you to jail. If you told us where the money was hid, me and Teddy would talk to the sheriff," Bobby said.

"Don't tell them, Joanie!" Stevie screamed, jumping to his feet. "They ain't about to send a bunch of kids to jail. All we have to do is act like we are scared and real sorry for what we done."

"Fat chance, kid," Bobby said, shaking his head. "You don't know old man Wiesmulluer very well. He's meaner than you can believe. He ain't about to let you off the hook just because you're youngsters. Why, if you don't tell him where his money is hid, he's liable to get a knife and lop off your ears!" Bobby told them and made a chopping motion with his hand.

"Ha! You don't scare me," Stevie said and hooted.

Bobby's threats might not have scared Junior, but it sure put the fear into his little sister. She let out a high-pitched scream that sent the hairs on the back of my neck shooting straight up. Slapping her hands over her ears, she hid behind Joan. "Joanie, don't let them cut my ears off."

"Don't worry, Jenny. I won't let them hurt you," Joan promised, putting her arm around the little tyke.

"Come on, Jenny, you can tell me where the money is," I coaxed, holding out my finger to tickle her nose.

"I ain't telling!" she screamed and promptly bit my finger.

Bobby laughed so hard I thought he would cry. "Aw, let's forget about that and get back to town. Let old man Wiesmulluer deal with them," Bobby suggested. "I'm about ready to drop in my tracks."

They didn't want to go, but we weren't in the mood for any back talk. We just bundled them kids up and slapped them on their horses. We had to put up with a lot of screeching and screaming from Junior and the little girl, but we drug the whole pack of them into town. Joan didn't say a word, she just kept looking at me out of the corner of her eye. I sure hoped she wasn't planning anything. My head couldn't take much more.

As we rode back into town, it surprised me to see lights blazing in the hotel. We put the horses up, then hurried over there. Eddy sat in the lobby waiting on us, the others having all gone to bed.

When she saw them little girls, Eddy let out a squeal, rushing over to them. She fussed over them, hugging them and pushing the hair out of their faces.

"If you two think you can handle this bunch of desperadoes by yourselves, I'll go on up to bed," Bobby announced, yawning as he climbed the stairs. "See you in the morning."

"Joan and Jenny can stay in my room," Eddy said, handing me a key. "Stevie can sleep with you."

I made a face as I took the key. I didn't like getting stuck with the little runt. "Let's go, Junior," I said wearily, giving him a little shove toward the stairs.

Surprisingly, he went upstairs without a fight. He dropped into the bed and fell asleep almost immediately. I had to smile as I took his boots off. Despite all he'd done to us, Stevie was still just a little boy, and a mighty tired one at that.

I reckon I was tired too. I jerked off my boots, then collapsed in the bed beside him. It seemed like I barely got to sleep when a thunderous fist pounded on my door. I stumbled out of bed, tripping over one of Stevie's boots. Cursing, I kicked the boot under the bed and swung the door open.

A smiling Weeb greeted me as I pulled the door open. "Dang, boy, was you planning to sleep the whole day away?" he asked cheerfully.

"Yesterday was a long day," I answered grumpily.

"I reckon, but it's over now. Time to get up and around. Sheriff Len wants to see you."

"How is he?" I asked, feeling ashamed that I hadn't thought to ask earlier.

Weeb shrugged. ''He's worrying again. I reckon that's a good sign. He said he wanted to have a few words with you.''

''All right, I'm coming.'' While Weeb waited, I pulled on my boots and slung my gunbelt over my shoulder. I took a last look over my shoulder at Stevie. The boy was still sleeping, so I figured he would be all right till I got back.

Sheriff Len sat in a cot at the doctor's office, propped up by a huge pillow. ''Sheriff Cooper, I need to ask a favor of you,'' he said as we came through the door. His voice sounded weak, but his eyes were bright and alert.

''Sure, anything you want,'' I promised immediately.

Sheriff Len smiled weakly and shook his head. ''You might want to hear me out before you agree,'' he said.

''Boy, that's for sure,'' Weeb chortled.

''What do you want?'' I asked, an uneasy feeling creeping up my spine.

''I want you to find Riley Hunt and arrest him.''

I frowned, rubbing my chin as I sat down on the edge of the bunk. ''I don't know,'' I said slowly. ''I don't know if I could do that.''

''Why not? You're a sheriff, aren't you?'' Sheriff Len asked.

''Yeah, sure,'' I said hastily and felt my face burn. ''It's just that we have a herd of cattle down in Arizona to pick up and take to Wyoming, and we're running out of time. We'll be lucky to get them home before the snow flies as it is."

"Sure," Len said, his voice sounding dejected. "I realize that you have your own problems, but I'm asking you for a favor, one lawman to another. Your friends could start on without you. Once Hunt is captured, you could join them." Sheriff Len grabbed my arm. "I know something of Hunt. The man's a killer. I'm afraid he might come back."

"I'll think about it," I promised.

"How about the money? Has it been recovered?" he asked, and I shook my head. "The folks of this town can't afford to lose that money."

"I'd like to help you," I said. I stood up and walked over to the window. "We can help you get the money back. After all, we can't leave until we get our own stakes back. As for chasing after Riley Hunt, I'll have to speak to my friends about that."

"Of course," Len said, looking pleased. "Just don't take too long. Riley Hunt is a dangerous man. He isn't going to take what happened lying down. I fear what he might do."

His words worrying a hole in my mind, I stepped out of the doctor's house. I hadn't walked ten paces before Joanie cornered me. "Eddy sent me to find you. She said if you wanted something to eat, you best come to the café."

I thought it over, but it didn't take long for me to make up my mind. "Let's go," I said, ready to eat a whole cow.

"I have something for you," she said, holding her hands behind her back and ducking her head.

"What is it?" I asked, my voice sounding gruffer than I meant it to be.

"Here," she said and pressed something into my hand. "It's a knife. Do you like it?"

I looked at the small clasp knife in my hand and recognized it immediately. It was the knife that Marie Wiesmulluer gave to her husband for Christmas several years ago. "Yeah, it's real nice," I said and hurriedly stuffed it into my pocket before old man Wiesmulluer saw it. He set store by that knife, and would have a conniption if he saw it. "You know, Joanie, if you wanted to do something for me, you could tell me where you kids hid the money and the rest of our stuff."

"I can't do that," Joanie said, looking up at me with wide, serious eyes. "Stevie made me promise not to tell. It isn't right to make a promise and then break it. My mother taught me that."

"Didn't she teach you that it wasn't right to steal?" I asked grumpily.

Joanie smiled brightly. "I guess she might have mentioned it. But starving isn't very good either." With that Joanie ran ahead, leaving me to wonder what in the devil that was all about. Oh, well, it wasn't important, surely not as important as the food waiting for me in the café. Picking up my feet, I hustled down the street.

Breakfast, or dinner I guess you'd have to call it, since it was way past noon, turned out to be an awkward, strained affair. The women seemed at ease, eating and chatting like a flock of magpies. They fussed and fretted over them danged kids, totally ignoring us men. When one of the women did speak to us, she was extra polite.

We didn't mind much. Long as they wasn't raking us up one side and down the other, we was happy to eat in peace. Still, all that politeness could get on a body's nerves after a while. It was like setting on a keg of blasting powder, just wondering when the darned thing was going to go off. You knew it would, just not when.

It was that danged Bobby Stamper who went and lit the fuse. "I reckon you women will be heading back to Whiskey City tomorrow. If you like, we could arrange for Abner and Weeb to go with you."

Well that did it. I swear, the sound of his words was like the sight of a red flag to a bull. Four pairs of ice cold eyes swung over at Bobby, staring him down like so many rifle barrels.

"We thought you would be coming back with us," Marie Wiesmulluer said.

"We got a herd of cattle to go get and bring back with us," Bobby said, fanning the flames. I swear, if

I coulda reached him, I woulda belted him. Didn't the fool know when to let well enough alone?

"Isn't it getting late in the year for that now?" Betsy asked. She looked at Bobby, a frown on her creamy face. "You told me you'd have to rush to get the herd before winter and you've wasted several days here."

"Bah," old man Wiesmulluer said, whacking the table with his open hand. "We'll bring that herd through if I have to hogtie them and pull them through the snow on a sled," he allowed.

"Be serious, there just isn't time to go fetch that herd. Face it, you'll just have to wait until next year," Marie pointed out.

"Perhaps the women have a point. I'm not sure this drive was such a good idea. Perhaps we should wait. Besides, my crops need tending," Mr. Claude worried.

"Sheriff Len wants me to help him capture Riley Hunt," I said suddenly. I could tell by the stunned looks on their faces that they were shocked. I don't know what surprised them more, the fact that Len asked for my help or that I was considering giving it to him.

Eddy frowned and shot me a frosty look out of the corner of her eyes. "What do you know about tracking down a killer like Riley Hunt?" she scoffed.

I straightened up, glaring down my nose at her. "I'll have you know that I am a sheriff. I know what I am doing. I reckon I can handle Riley Hunt."

Eddy slammed her cup down, slopping coffee on the tablecloth. "You'd get yourself killed is what you'd do."

"That's right," Wiesmulluer said, rolling his eyes and acting like he thought I had went off the deep end. "We haven't got time for such foolishness. We got a herd of cattle in Arizona to pick up."

That started the argument all over again. While the others tried to hash out a settlement, Eddy jerked me off to one side. "Teddy, I've been thinking about those kids," she said, her eyes bright and shiny. She paused like she expected me to say something, but I didn't even want to think about them brats, much less talk about them. "I was thinking," she started again, and I groaned, a sneaky suspicion of what she had in mind growing inside me. "Those children need a home. We could take them in and give them a home," she said, practically jumping up and down with the idea.

All of a sudden, I felt like I had been slugged in the gut, and truthfully, I would have preferred the punch. "Look, Eddy, we ain't in any position to take in a raft of kids. We ain't even married ourselves yet."

"That's no big deal," Eddy said assuringly, waving a hand at me. "Preacher Tom would marry us today if we asked him to."

"I don't know," I said slowly while my mind raced. "Ol' Tom's wounded. A weddin' is a powerful thing. I doubt if he's up to doing one,'' I said desperately.

''Oh, pooh. He was only shot in the shoulder,'' Eddy spoofed, patting my chest. ''Why, he's already up and around. I saw him and Bertha hitching up a buggy this morning.''

''Oh, well, then, he's likely too busy,'' I said as she crossed her arms and tapped her foot on the floor. ''Besides, we don't even have a house ourselves. Where would we keep those kids?''

All of a sudden, I wanted the company and support of the other men. Eyeing her warily, I began to edge back to the table. ''You just don't like them, that's all. After you get to know them, you'll see they are fine young people,'' Eddy said, following me.

''What about me staying to help Sheriff Len?'' I countered, sliding in beside Bobby. ''You'd have a hard time handling a bunch of kids by yourself.''

Eddy's eyes flew open and her foot froze in midtap. Fire blazing in her black eyes, she placed her hands on her hips and glared at me. ''I thought we already settled that. You're not going after that awful man and that's final.''

''Well, I *am* going and there ain't no way you can stop me!'' I declared. As usual, I was talking without using my brain, but right then I was upset and didn't care.

"You must be very brave," Joanie said, looking at me all bigeyed and dopey. "I've heard that Riley Hunt is a vicious killer."

"You heard!" Wiesmulluer exploded, spitting coffee all over the place. His face hard as a Montana winter, he slapped his cup down on the table. "You claimed Hunt was your father," he said accusingly as Stevie kicked his sister under the table.

"We just said that so you would be scared of us," little Jenny said brightly.

Eddy let out a squeal, laying her head on my shoulder and squeezing my arm. "Isn't she just darling?"

Now, if I were cornered into being downright truthful, I'd have to admit that that little girl was cute as a june bug. Still, I didn't want to take her home. For one thing, I was still trying to figure out Eddy. In less than a heartbeat she went from being mad at me to cooing at that little girl. I don't reckon I'll ever figure out that woman, and I sure didn't need a pack of rug rats hanging around who were crazier still.

"If Riley Hunt wasn't your father, what happened to your parents?" Claude asked.

"Our pa left one day and never came back. After a few days our ma went looking for him and she never came back," Stevie answered with a shrug, like it didn't matter, but I could tell from the look on his face that it mattered a lot.

"Indians got them," Wiesmulluer said.

"It doesn't matter what happened to their parents. What matters now is that we do what's best for the children," Marie said evenly. One thing about Marie, she was a level-headed woman; 'course, she had to be to keep a rein on the hot-blooded Wiesmulluer.

"They need a home, and I think me and Teddy are the best ones to give it to them," Eddy said promptly.

"Come on Eddy," I said. "It isn't that I don't want to help the little tykes, but I just don't see how we could possibly take them on right now."

"For once, you're talking sense," Wiesmulluer said, grumbling.

"Besides, I'm going to help Sheriff Len catch Riley Hunt."

"Well, that didn't last long," Wiesmulluer said, throwing his hands in the air.

"Somebody has to put a stop to the man, and Sheriff Len isn't up to the job," I argued.

It was shaping up to be one heck of a scuddle, when Bertha and Preacher Tom burst through the door like a runaway train. "Guess what?" Bertha shouted loud enough to rattle the crockery. Before we had a chance to even recover our hearing, much less take a stab at what she was blabbering about, her and Tom up and told us. "We're getting married!" they shouted together.

For a second, nobody did anything but hold their ears. It was Mrs. Claude who found her voice first. "That's very nice. Congratulations to you both. We're very happy for you,'' she said quietly. ''But right now, we're trying to decide what to do with the kids. They need a home.''

Bertha smiled down at them. ''That shouldn't be a problem. I've known these kids for a long time. They are such sweet kids. Anyone would be proud to have them,'' she said.

''Well what about you and Tom?'' I asked quickly. ''You two are going to make a home. You need some kids.''

Bertha frowned, biting her fingernail. ''Children would be nice,'' she cooed, looking coyly at Tom.

''I don't know. That one shot at me,'' he said, pointing a finger at Stevie.

''I did not!'' Junior sputtered. ''If I had shot at you, you wouldn't still be walking around.''

''They're spirited, but they're good kids,'' I said ''All they need is a firm hand on the reins.''

''I don't know,'' Tom said, slowly backing away as the women advanced on him. ''I was looking forward to spending some time alone with Bertha.''

Blowing out a sigh, I smiled to myself. That poor man didn't have a chance. I picked up my coffee cup, a feeling of relief washing over me. That feeling didn't last long.

I was just getting ready to take a sip of my coffee when Joanie slid down the bench beside me. ''How come you don't like us?'' she asked, squeezing my arm.

Her question startled me, and I sucked a sight bigger charge of that coffee than I intended, scalding the devil out of my mouth. Before I had a chance to answer, the little one, Jenny, crawled right up on the table and grabbed the front of my shirt. "Yeah. How come you don't like us? We like you!" she yelled in my face.

"I like you fine," I mumbled, holding my scalded lips.

Joanie hitched a little closer, looking up at me with those big brown eyes. "Then why don't you want us to come live with you?"

"Yeah, buster. How come?" Jenny shouted, tugging on the front of my shirt.

There's some things a man just can't be expected to take. I mean, I'll ride the meanest horse around. Shoot, I'd even crawl down in a well filled with rattlers, but set there with them kids swarming all over me? Well, that's more than a body could be expected to take. I jumped out of my chair and shot out the door like I'd been fired from a cannon. I didn't stop running till I was safely hid in the barn.

A half hour later, I was still cowering behind a stack of straw, trying to steady my nerves, when my friends came in the barn. "Where are you fellers going?" I asked as they saddled their horses.

"The kid finally told us where he hid the money. "We're going to get it," Bobby answered.

"I'll go with you," I shouted, feeling the need for open spaces.

We rode out of town and followed Stevie's directions to a tee, but we didn't find the money. All we found at the end of the trail was the carcass of a dead coyote. Wiesmulluer ground his teeth and his face turned so red that I thought his hat was going to blow clean off his head. Growling and muttering, he chewed on his reins, biting them hard enough to tear a chunk loose.

"*Mon Dieu*! He lied to us!" Mr. Claude shouted, looking almost as mad as Wiesmulluer. "That boy needs a trip behind the woodshed," he said growling.

Even Bobby, who usually saw the humor in everything, threw his hat down on the ground, then jumped down and kicked it several times.

I tried to get worked up about the money, but couldn't quite pull it off. All of a sudden, the money didn't seem like much of a big deal. As a grim-jawed Wiesmulluer jerked his horse around and started for town, I followed slowly.

It was way past dark when we reached town, but that didn't stop Wiesmulluer from storming the hotel like Sherman going into Atlanta. He practically ripped the door loose from the wall as he burst into the lobby. He stopped just inside the door, his chest heaving. "Where is that little spit wad?" he roared.

The lobby was empty except for Marie Wiesmulluer, who sat in a chair, reading a book. As her husband glared at her, breathing like a steam engine, she slowly closed the book. "The children are upstairs, sleeping."

"Well, go get that boy. He lied to us about the money," Wiesmulluer raged.

Marie slapped that book down on a table and put her hands on her hips. "I will not. That little boy needs his rest. Talk about that money can wait until morning," she said sternly.

"No it won't! I want to see him right now!" Wiesmulluer shouted, stomping in circles around the lobby.

"You can't go get the money until morning anyway. So there's no sense in rousing the boy out of his bed. You can speak to him tomorrow," Marie argued.

Wiesmulluer glared at his wife for a long time, then his shoulders sagged. "All right," he grumbled, giving in. "But come morning, I'm going to get the truth out of that little stinkbug." He stomped up the stairs, still muttering to himself. I can tell you one thing—come morning, I wouldn't want to be in little Stevie's shoes.

I trooped up the stairs behind him, more than ready for the end of this day. I eased into my room carefully, and like Marie said, Junior was asleep. Moving quietly, I took off my boots and slipped into bed. The last thing I needed was to talk to another kid today.

I was plumb tuckered and I must have slept like a hibernating bear. I didn't hear Stevie ease out of bed and slip out of the room.

I woke with a feeling that everything wasn't as it should be. Rolling over, I sat on the edge of the bed, holding my aching head. It took me a few seconds to realize Stevie was gone!

Chapter Twelve

I snapped to my feet like I had a spring in the seat of my britches. For a few seconds, I stood in the middle of the room, glancing wildly about me, hoping to find the little runt curled up on the floor. When I knew he was for sure gone, my first thought was how I could explain just how he managed to slip away from me. Maybe, I could find the little bugger and fetch him back before anyone realized he'd even been gone. One look out the window told me that wasn't going to work. Already, the sky was beginning to lighten, a sure sign that morning was almost on us. It wouldn't be long till folks rolled out of their beds. And if I knew Wiesmulluer, he'd make a beeline here, with every intention of shaking Stevie till the boy fessed up to what he did with our money.

The money!

Stevie wouldn't run away without the money. The more I thought about it, the more convinced I became that Stevie was on his way to the place he stashed the money.

Grabbing my boots in one hand and my gunbelt in the other, I slipped out of the room. I eased down the hall to the room where Eddy and the girls were staying. With a look both ways, I rapped on the door.

I pressed my ear to the door, listening for movement inside. I couldn't hear a sound from inside, so I knocked again, louder this time. I heard a muffled sound, then the bed creaked. In a few seconds, Eddy opened the door, and she didn't look any too happy at being woke up.

"Teddy, what are you doing? It isn't even morning yet," she said, clutching her faded robe around her.

"Never mind that. I gotta talk to Joan," I said, and looked back over my shoulder to make sure no one else had woke up.

Well, Eddy put her foot down. "Teddy, those girls have been through a lot. They need their rest. Whatever you have on your mind can wait until morning." She started to close the door.

"Eddy, wait," I pleaded. She stopped but I could tell from her expression that she wanted an explanation. Well, so much for keeping this under my hat. "It's Stevie. He took off during the night."

Eddy tilted her head, giving me a severe look. ''What do you mean, he took off? Weren't you watching him?''

''Well, no. Actually, I was sleeping. I reckon he played possum until I went to sleep, then he snuck out,'' I explained hurriedly. ''I figure he'll head straight to the place where they hid the money. I need Joan to tell me where that is so I can go fetch him.''

A doubtful frown crossed Eddy's face, but she stepped back, letting me into the room. Both girls were awake, lying side by side with the covers pulled up to their chins.

''This better not be some fool scheme of yours to trick them into telling you where the money is,'' Eddy warned in a hissing voice.

Pasting her with a superior look, I sat down on the bed beside the girls. ''Joan, I need you to tell me where the money is hid.''

Before Joan could answer, Jenny sat straight up, tugging at my sleeve. ''Mr. Cooper, Mr. Cooper,'' she cried.

''Not now, Jenny,'' I said, smiling down at her and patting her blonde curls. ''This is very important. I need to ask your sister a few questions. Then you can talk, okay?''

Jenny wrinkled up her nose in disgust and crossed her arms, but she stayed quiet. ''Now, Joanie, where did you hide the money?''

Jenny yanked on my sleeve. "Mr. Cooper, your boots stink. They are making me sick."

"Okay, I'll put them on," I growled as I tugged them on.

"Mr. Cooper, you should comb your hair," Jenny said, running her fingers through my hair and yanking some of it out. "Our mama always said you should comb your hair every morning."

"I was in a hurry," I snapped.

Jenny stood up in the bed, put her little hands on her hips and gave me a stern look. "That's no excuse."

"I'll tend to it in a minute," I promised, ignoring Eddy's laugh. I turned my attention to Joan. "Look, Stevie has run away. I figure he will head to where you hid the money. I need to find him and bring him back before something happens to him."

Joan hesitated, looking to Eddy for support. "Go ahead, dear. Tell him," Eddy encouraged.

"My mother had a cabin. We hid the money in the back of the fireplace. There's a rock you can pull out and hide stuff behind."

"Where's the cabin at?" I asked, listening intently as Joan gave me the directions. I didn't care for the place she described; it was dangerously close to Riley Hunt's hideout. Even after all my talk about going after the outlaw, I really didn't want to bump into the man.

When she finished, I smiled at them and stood up. "Don't worry about your brother. I'll find him and bring him back."

"I'm going with you," Eddy announced, her face determined.

I knew it wouldn't do a lot of good, but I tried to talk her out of the notion. "That's not a good idea. I can travel faster by myself," I argued, but Eddy's only response was to place her hands on her hips and tap her foot. "Besides, somebody should stay with these girls."

That argument wiped the smug expression off Eddy's face, replaced quickly by a thoughtful one. She puckered her lips, but didn't say a word as I ducked my head and scooted to the door. "Mr. Cooper," Joan called as my hand closed on the door knob. "Be careful, Mr. Cooper. I wouldn't be able to stand it if anything happened to you."

Startled and more than a little taken back by the emotion in her voice, I hesitated. "Uh, yeah. I'll be real careful," I promised and darted out the door.

As I hurried down the street, the sky began to turn pink and lights blazed in the windows of a few houses. Since I wanted to get out of town before anyone knew what I was up to, I hustled over to the stable. I'd just got my saddle buckled on my horse when Eddy skidded into the barn. She was dressed in riding clothes and out of breath. "Saddle a horse for me. I'm going with you."

''What about the girls? Do you think they should be left alone? I don't reckon that's a good idea.''

Eddy gave me a dose of the smile she always wore when she was about to pull something over on me. ''I woke Mother. She's watching them,'' she said haughtily. ''Now, move your caboose and saddle me a horse.''

''You didn't wake your father, did you?'' I asked, slapping a saddle on her horse.

She laughed, tweaking my nose lightly. ''What's the matter, Teddy? Don't you want everyone to know that you were outsmarted by a ten-year-old boy?''

''Aw, shut up and get on your horse,'' I muttered, and gave her a shove to help her aboard.

''My, aren't we touchy this morning,'' Eddy said, laughing brightly.

We rode side by side as our horses shuffled slowly out of town. I could feel Eddy glancing at me out of the corner of her eye, but I ignored that. ''You've got an admirer,'' she said with a sly smirk.

I kept my eyes pointed straight ahead and pretended like I never even heard. From vivid experience, I knew that when Eddy used that tone she had some kind of misery in store for me. I told myself to keep looking straight ahead and keep my mouth shut. No, sir, I wasn't about to fall into her trap. That's what I told myself, but I couldn't do 'er. I just had to ask. ''What do you mean, admirer?''

‘‘Joan,’’ Eddy said brightly. ‘‘She has a crush on you.’’

‘‘Aw, she does not,’’ I mumbled and squirmed in the saddle.

‘‘Oh, yes, she does. She talked about you for a long time last night.’’

‘‘Did she tell you that she smacked me over the head? Twice!’’ I asked sourly.

Eddy laughed delightfully. ‘‘Yes, and she felt just terrible about that. She even cried. You should be ashamed of yourself, making her cry.’’

‘‘Well, I durn near cried when she walloped me, so I reckon that makes us even,’’ I shot back, rubbing my head. ‘‘I still got lumps! I reckon it’s a good thing she likes me so all fired much; otherwise, she’d likely killed me.’’

‘‘Your head is hard. I doubt if anything could dent it,’’ Eddy replied, and I could tell she was enjoying this. ‘‘I told her not to worry, that you deserved just what you got. Now, when we get back, you be nice to her. Them kids have been through a lot, losing their mother and all.’’

‘‘Okay, I’ll be nice,’’ I promised, but what I figured to do was avoid her.

Eddy rocked in her saddle, a sad expression on her face. ‘‘I’m going to miss those kids,’’ she said softly.

‘‘Huh? What do you mean, miss them? I thought Preacher Tom and Bertha was going to take them on.’’

"They are," Eddy said. "But they are going to stay here in Miles City."

I clenched my fist, shaking it in happiness. As soon as we drug Junior back to town, I wouldn't have to see them kids anymore.

Hours later, we rode into the canyon Joan described. A couple of miles up the canyon, we found the cabin. We drew up a few yards from the shack. The lone window in the sorry affair was broken, a tattered curtain fluttering in the breeze. The door sagged crazily from one hinge, and a huge hole gaped in the roof. "They lived here?" Eddy asked, wrinkling her nose at the dirt floor.

"I guess so. Come on. Let's get the money and go."

"What about Stevie?" Eddy reminded me. "Isn't he the reason we are here?"

I frowned, making a face. Just the mention of that little water dog was enough to put me in a foul mood. "Oh, sure, we'll grab him, but we might as well get the money while we're here," I said hurriedly.

"Is he here? I don't see him or his horse," Eddy said, glancing around.

"He must be," I grunted as I dropped down from my horse. "I've been seeing his tracks all the way out here. I reckon he's inside," I added as I helped her down.

I kicked the cabin door open, and it promptly fell off its hinges, raising a dust cloud big enough to choke a hippo. Waving the dust away, I stepped inside. One look was enough to know Stevie wasn't inside. The cabin had only one room, which was bare except for a table and one broken chair. There wasn't any place he could hide.

"Where is he?" Eddy asked, placing her hand on my shoulder as she peered past me.

"I don't know," I mumbled. I tossed the table aside and dropped to the dirt floor in front of the fireplace. I reached inside, using my knife to pry out the stones. I found the compartment without any trouble, but I didn't find the money.

"Come on, Teddy, hurry up. Get the money and let's go. I don't like it here. Besides, I'm worried about Stevie."

"I can't find it," I said and crawled plumb inside the fireplace. I lit a match, holding it up to the cubbyhole. The money was gone! I heard Eddy mumble something behind me, her voice muffled by the fireplace. "What?" I hollered.

Eddy didn't answer. Danged woman was always doing that, not answering me, I mean. Grumbling under my breath, I backed out of the fireplace. As I turned around, I saw there was a good reason why she didn't answer. A man had his arm around her throat and a hand over her mouth.

Besides the man holding Eddy, another man leaned insolently in the doorway. While I didn't know their names, I recognized them as Riley Hunt's men.

Chapter Thirteen

The man holding Eddy grinned as he took his hand from her mouth and drew his gun. ''Drop your guns, big man,'' he said, and ground his pistol into her side.

I didn't want to do it. The moment I surrendered my guns, we would be completely at their mercy. I really didn't think he would shoot her. Even outlaws hesitated before they harmed a woman. I'd bet there were men at the hideout who would kill him if he hurt Eddy.

Deep in my heart, I knew he wouldn't shoot her, but I looked at the pleading in her eyes and I couldn't take that chance. ''If I throw down my guns, let the girl go.''

The two exchanged grins, which I didn't trust. ''Sure, we'll let her go. Won't we, Walt?'' the man in the doorway promised, and Walt nodded, but he didn't quit grinding the pistol into Eddy's side.

I wasn't nowhere near convinced. I didn't trust either of them any farther than I could throw a purple ox, but I had very little choice. Working slowly, I unbuckled my gunbelt, hesitating just an instant before I let it fall. As soon as the gunbelt hit the floor, the man in the doorway jumped forward and snatched it off the floor.

"The boss has been looking forward to seeing you again. He ain't forgot that whupping you laid on him. It'd likely be a kindness if we was to kill you right here and now."

"Well, don't do me any favors," I grumbled.

"Don't worry. We wasn't figuring on it," Walt said, laughing in my face. " 'Course, you may be singing a different tune once Riley gets his hands on you," he added. Shifting his grip on Eddy, he jerked his head in the direction of the door. "Jim, go bring the horses around."

"You said you would let her go," I reminded.

"Well, I lied," Walt jeered. "I'm starting to get real attached to the young lady. I reckon we'll just take her along to keep us company." He kept his arm around Eddy, dragging her with him as he backed to the door. He looked briefly outside, then back at me. "Okay, big boy, get outside."

My whole body shaking with rage, I stalked outside. Walt drug Eddy out behind me, then shoved her roughly toward her horse. ''Mount up, sweetie, we're going for a little ride.''

They took us back to Hunt's hideout, and as we rode into the outlaw's canyon, a feeling of hopelessness crashed over me. Last time we came here, we'd barely gotten out with our lives. I had a feeling getting out this time was going to be harder, a lot harder. 'Course, they might just carry us out—in a pine box.

They herded us straight to the saloon, shoving us roughly inside. Just like last time, Luther stood behind the bar. The sight of Luther gave me a ray of hope. Luther was Bobby's friend and didn't seem to have any love for Riley Hunt. Maybe the bald outlaw would help us.

''You two, park it over there,'' Walt said, pointing with his rifle to a table. ''Jim, go fetch Riley.''

Walt placed his rifle on the bar and drew his pistol. ''Luther, give me a beer,'' he said, pointing the pistol in our direction.

Luther slid a beer down the bar down to him, then drew another. He carried that beer and a pitcher and extra glass to our table.

''Hey, don't give them anything,'' Walt shouted, but Luther paid him no mind.

He sat the beer in front of me, then poured the other glass full from the pitcher. ''Here, have some lemonade, miss,'' he said.

"Thanks, Luther," I said, gratefully taking a sip. "Luther, this is Eddy," I said, then glanced at Eddy. "Luther is one of Bobby's friends."

Eddy smiled up at Luther. "Glad to meet you, sir. Thank you for the lemonade."

Luther's rough face colored a little as he traced circles on the table with his finger. "You're welcome," he said, then looked into my eyes. "Did Bobby send you here to square his debt?"

"Not exactly," I hedged nervously. "But Bobby's real concerned about that. I'm sure he'll be paying the money real soon."

"Yeah, I bet," Luther said with a growl. "I don't suppose there's any chance you can pay for these drinks?"

"Certainly," Eddy said, and dug the money from her pocket.

Luther started to take the money, then shook his head. "Aw, you keep it. I'll put these on Bobby's tab." He glanced at me. "I like her," he said, and crossed back to the bar.

"Ain't that sweet?" Walt jeered. "I wouldn't get too attached to them. I don't think they'll be around for long."

Walt's words took the flavor right out of my beer, but I wasn't going to get a chance to enjoy it anyway. Riley Hunt stormed into the saloon like a tornado with a bad attitude. He didn't bother to say howdy or doody, he just marched up to me and belted me in the mouth.

The force of the blow knocked my chair over and sent me skidding across the floor. A roaring sound filled my ears as I lunged to my feet. I drew back my fist, ready to give as good as I got. The trouble was, Riley was ready for me. Just as I got my feet planted under me, he splattered me again. This one didn't put me down, but it watered my eyes and man did it hurt.

Roaring in pain, I grabbed Riley's throat with both hands and squeezed with all my might. I figured I'd either choke him down or pop his head clean off his shoulders, and right then I didn't care which.

Eddy screamed a warning, and out of the corner of my eye, I saw Walt leap away from the bar, pointing his pistol at us. I knew he couldn't shoot for fear of hitting Hunt, so I didn't figure he was a threat. But Walt had other ideas. Instead of shooting, he slugged me in the kidneys with the butt of his revolver. A wave of pain raced up my spine, but I held onto Hunt with a death grip.

Walt smashed the pistol in my side twice more; slowly my grip weakened and my legs buckled. Riley and I both ended up on our knees, gasping for air. Hunt recovered first, lurching to his feet. "I'm going to kill you for that!" he roared, his voice hoarse. He kicked me in the side, then hollered at Walt. "Put him in the chair."

I clutched my side as Walt hauled me to my feet and shoved me into the chair. Despite the pain in my side, I forced myself to sit up straight. I didn't want to give them the satisfaction of knowing they had hurt me.

Hunt paced in front of me, gently massaging his throat. I took more than a little satisfaction at seeing the red welts on his neck, which were already turning purple around the edges. By morning, his whole neck was going to be black and blue. As I watched Hunt with guarded eyes, I saw Chub slip through the front door and quietly take a seat.

Hunt stopped suddenly. He leaned in close, resting his hands on the arms of the chair. "You're a dead man," he said, his voice still raspy. "The only question is how you die—quick and painless, or slow. Real slow."

I felt a shiver race through my body and a nerve jumped in my eye, but I kept my voice level. "What do you want?"

Hunt leaned in closer until his nose almost touched my face. "What I want is the money you took from me. Give me that, and I'll kill you real quick. Otherwise, I'll take my knife and start cutting off chunks until you do talk," he threatened, and to back up his threats, he pulled out his knife and showed it to me.

I gripped the arms of the chair to keep the shakes in my hands from showing. My eyes locked onto Hunt's knife as he tested the edge with his thumb. I wanted to look away. My whole body screamed for me to knock him aside and run, but I couldn't move a muscle. Nor could I tear my eyes away from that gleaming knife. With almost morbid fascination they followed the razor-sharp blade as Hunt twirled it in front of my face.

"Not talking?" he asked. "Well, you will," he said confidently then flicked the blade under my eye. I felt the cold steel blade slice my skin, but I still couldn't move. All I could do was stare at the drop of blood on the tip of the knife. Hunt stepped back, a furious expression clouding his face. "So you like pain?" he hissed, stepping around the table. He stood behind Eddy, stroking the top of her head. "Maybe she does too?"

Eddy elbowed him in the leg, but Hunt only laughed. He grabbed her hair in his left hand, cruelly jerking her head back. He held the knife in his right hand, bringing it down toward her throat.

All of a sudden, my muscles knew how to work and I sprang out of my chair like a charging lion. "I'm gonna rip you to shreds, you . . ."

I never got to finish, because Walt jumped me from behind. He wrapped his arm around my throat, shutting off my wind. Like a fish fighting the hook, I threshed from side to side, but I couldn't throw him loose. I tried to reach back and grab his hair or gouge his eyes, but I couldn't reach. As my strength ebbed from lack of air, tears streamed down my face. This man was going to hurt Eddy, hurt her bad, and I couldn't do anything to stop him.

I couldn't help her, but Luther could. His short club clenched in his hand, he stalked around the bar. He pointed the club at Hunt, his whole body looking like black clouds rolling in. "You let her go, or I'm going to tear your head off!"

Riley let go of Eddy's hair. "This ain't none of your business, Luther. You don't want to get involved."

"I'm warning you . . . ," Luther started, but Hunt's vicious laugh cut him off.

"You're warning me?" Hunt asked softly. "What are you going to do, Luther?" With a flick of his wrist, Hunt flipped the knife at Luther. The blade stuck in the floor between Luther's feet. As the knife quivered, Riley's hand fell to his gun.

Walt leaned forward to watch the action, and his grip around my throat slacked enough that I could drag some air into my searing lungs.

"What are you going to do?" Riley repeated. His fingers tickling the butt of his pistol, he took a step forward.

Too late, I guess Luther realized he should have brought a gun instead of that club. The club slipped from his fingers as his eyes darted around the room. They opened wide as he spied Walt's rifle resting on the bar. He jumped at the rifle, moving with incredible quickness for a man his size. As quick as he moved, Riley Hunt moved even faster.

Lunging across the room, Hunt drew his pistol and slashed down viciously at Luther's head. The barrel of that pistol caught Luther behind the ear and ripped an angry gash in his bare scalp. Without a word, the big man crashed to the floor, dragging the rifle off the bar. Luther was a tough man and he wasn't ready to give up. He reached feebly for the rifle, but Riley stamped the back of his hand.

Grinding his boot heel into the back of Luther's hand, Hunt contemptuously holstered his gun and picked up the rifle. He smiled back at us, then smashed the butt of the rifle into Luther's head. Luther's body twitched once, then lay completely still.

Hunt tossed the rifle behind the bar, then smiled wickedly at Eddy. ''Now, where were we?'' he asked, reaching for the knife stuck in the floor.

''Hold it, Riley!'' Chub called, his chair scraping against the floor as he jumped to his feet. Chub's face was chalky as a corpse's, but his teeth were clenched determinedly. ''You ain't gonna hurt that girl!'' Chub squeaked, his shaky hand hovering over his pistol.

''Chub, you idiot, get out of here right now and I'll forget about this,'' Riley said and took a step at Eddy.

''I ain't gonna do it, Riley,'' Chub said, sliding over a step to block Hunt. ''Hurting that girl ain't right and I ain't gonna let you do it.''

Riley Hunt threw back his head and laughed. His laughter stopped suddenly and his head snapped back down. His eyes shone bright as they bore into Chub.

At that moment, I knew Hunt was going to kill the little man.

I drove my elbow into Walt's stomach, throwing him off my back. Desperately, I dove at Hunt, but I was too late. With blurring speed, Hunt's hand snatched the pistol from the holster and fired two quick shots as the gun came level.

A split second too late, I crashed into Hunt. As I tackled Hunt, I heard the report of Chub's gun and felt something burning hot slap against my leg. We fell to the ground, with Hunt twisting away from me. He drove his fist into the side of my head, then surged to his feet.

He pointed his gun at me, and for a second, I just knew he would fire. Finally, he took a deep breath and relaxed. ''Walt, put your gun on him. If he moves again, shoot him in the other leg.''

Hunt turned to look at Chub, who lay on the floor, still, his arms flung wide. In two bounds, Hunt crossed to Chub, kicking the fallen man's foot. ''Stupid fool,'' he muttered.

All of a sudden, he whirled around and crossed to the bar. He grabbed a bottle off the shelf and took a long drink. He pulled the bottle away from his lips, staring at it for a long second. With a sudden burst of anger, he hurled the bottle into the row of bottles stacked on the back shelf. As the sound of shattered glass split the silence, Hunt bent over and pulled his knife from the floor. He rubbed the flat side of the blade against his cheek, looking at Eddy. The saloon was deathly still, the only sounds were the scrape of the knife on Hunt's cheeks and the slow drip of spilled whiskey dropping to the floor. Still rubbing his cheek, Hunt took a step toward Eddy.

Chapter Fourteen

"Wait a minute,'' I croaked, finally starting to use my head. ''I'll tell you where the money is.''

His back rigid as a tent pole, Hunt stopped, then turned slowly to face me. He wasn't wearing the look of satisfaction I expected. In fact, he looked vaguely disappointed. ''Where is it?'' he asked warily.

I sat up, looking down at the bullet hole in my leg, which was starting to bleed a lot. ''Stamper has it,'' I lied, using my bandanna to wrap my leg while I tried to come up with a story he might buy. ''He took off in the middle of the night with the money. We were looking for him when your men found us.''

''Where was he going?''

''I don't know,'' I said with a shrug. ''If I knew

where he was going, I'd already be there,'' I added hurriedly.

Hunt pursed his lips and stared at the ceiling. ''Nice try,'' he said, twirling the knife in his hands. ''I don't believe a word you just said. I reckon if I cut off one of the lady's fingers, you'd remember how to tell the truth quick enough.''

I couldn't think of a story he would believe, and I was real sure he'd never believe the truth. I'd suffered through it and I wasn't sure I believed it myself. Before I could think of what to say, a muffled shot sounded, followed by a barrage of gunfire.

''What the devil was that?'' Walt asked, springing away from the bar.

''That came from the canyon,'' Hunt said, looking out the door. ''It's Stamper!'' he exclaimed, whirling to face me. ''That's why you wouldn't talk. You knew he was coming to try and save you. Well, don't go getting your hopes up. He ain't gonna save you; he ain't even gonna be able to save himself. I'm going to take care of Stamper myself and then be right back to deal with you.''

Hunt started to go outside, but stopped at the door, pointing his finger back at Walt. ''You, stay here and keep an eye on them,'' he ordered; then he turned his eyes on me. ''When I get back, you better be ready to talk or else your pretty lady isn't going to be so pretty anymore.''

As Hunt went outside, I felt a surge of hope. Bobby was coming to rescue us! The hope didn't last. Bobby wasn't coming to save us. He didn't even know we was here. I didn't know who was shooting, but it wasn't Bobby.

Right then, I realized, no one was coming to save us. If we were going to get out of this, we had to do it on our own. Trying not to be obvious, I glanced about the room for something to use as a weapon. Only one man guarding us, this might be our best chance. Out of the corner of my eye, I spied Chub's gun lying beside his outstretched hand.

Walt wasn't paying a lot of attention to us. He kept craning his neck to look out the door. If I could get my hands on that gun . . .

My eyes shifted from Walt to that hogleg, measuring the distance between me and the weapon. A good eight to ten feet. A lot of ground to cover on a bum leg. I wasn't even sure the leg would support my weight.

I didn't think I had much of a chance, but I was going to go for it. Walt might miss his first shot, and even if he didn't I decided I'd rather go down scrapping and clawing than sitting on the floor.

As I gazed longingly at the pistol, I saw Chub's hand reach out for the weapon. I watched unbelievingly as he picked up the pistol and pointed it at Walt. Well, he didn't exactly point it at Walt, but he waved it in that general direction. He raised himself up a little then pulled the trigger. To my absolute shock, the bullet hit Walt in the legs, sweeping him off his feet.

I scurried across the floor, wanting to get my hands on Walt while he was still on the ground. It shames me to say that Eddy beat me to him; 'course I did have a bad leg. Eddy brought her chair with her, and, man, did she put it to good use. As Walt tried to rise, she set her feet and shattered the chair over his head.

He crashed back down, his head bouncing off the floor. He looked to be out, but I wasn't in the mood to take any chances. I latched onto his greasy hair and batted him in the whiskers.

While Eddy rushed over to Chub, I took a minute to catch my breath. I picked up Walt's gun, then hitched one-legged over to where Eddy knelt beside Chub. "How is he?" I asked.

Eddy glanced back over her shoulder, a hopeless look written on her face. "Did I get him?" Chub whispered, his thin chest rising and falling irregularly as he struggled to breathe.

"Yeah, you got him good," I said, squeezing his hand.

Chub smiled, a look of bliss settling on his face. "I never woulda dreamed I could beat him. I was so scared, but I knew it wasn't right." He looked at Eddy and took her hand. "All the time, I was so scared of him, but you're such a nice lady. I knew it wasn't right that he should hurt you. I never thought I could beat Riley. I don't reckon even Bobby could have done better.''

Eddy and I exchanged a glance, realizing Chub thought Hunt was the one he shot. I shrugged at the question in Eddy's eyes. I didn't have the heart to tell him the truth. Tears in her eyes, Eddy squeezed his hand.

''Don't cry, missy. It's all right, I ain't scared anymore,'' Chub murmured, wonder sounding in his voice. ''For the first time, I ain't scared.'' A fit of coughing racked Chub's body, his face twisted in pain. ''I stopped him, didn't I?''

''You sure did,'' I said, a lump in my throat.

Eddy pushed the hair back out of his face and caressed his cheek. ''You saved my life. I don't know how to thank you,'' she said, her voice husky.

Chub smiled, his breath and life seeming to leave his body in a long sigh. I held onto his hand for a long minute, then gently folded his hands across his chest.

''He saved our lives,'' Eddy whispered, tears streaming down her face.

''Yeah, I know,'' I said, with a catch in my voice. I put my arms around her, giving her a long hug. ''Let's not waste his effort. Go ahead and see about Luther while I try and figure a way out of this hole.''

Eddy dried the tears from her eyes, and with a final look at Chub she stood up. I picked Chub's pistol off the floor. I ejected the two spent shells, replacing them with fresh ones from Chub's shell belt.

I kept Walt's pistol in my hand and tucked Chub's behind my belt. Grabbing one of the poles that ran from the floor to the ceiling, I pulled myself to my feet. Hitching along, I crossed over to the door. Standing on my toes, I looked over the top of the batwing doors.

A cluster of men were grouped at the entrance of the canyon, pouring a steady stream of lead down the narrow cut. Nobody was coming up that canyon to save us. They'd be cut to shreds before they made it half way.

There wasn't any way we were going out that canyon either. I swore under my breath. As far as I knew, that was the only way in or out of this miserable hole.

I looked back at Eddy, who was bent over Luther with her to his chest. "How is he?"

"He's breathing!"

A glimmer of hope began to shine through the dark clouds of my despair. Maybe Luther knew of a back way out of this place. "Is he awake?" I asked excitedly, and Eddy shook her head.

I took a last look out the door, but nobody was paying any attention to the saloon. I started to turn, moving stiffly on my injured leg, when the back door of the saloon crashed open. I chopped down with my shooter, ready to blast whoever came through that door. I almost did, barely managing to hold my fire at the last instant.

Bobby Stamper lurched to a stop, skidding on the slick boards as he threw up his hands. ''Whoa, dead-eye, don't shoot. I came to get you out of here.''

''How did you even know we was here?'' I asked as I eased the hammer down on the pistol.

''Stevie,'' Bobby answered, lowering his hands, ''he saw Walt and Jim take you prisoner. That little runt came rushing into town with his backside on fire. He told us the whole story. Now, if old home week is over, can we get out of here?''

''We can't. Luther's been hurt,'' Eddy said.

Bobby bent down beside them. ''How bad is he?'' Bobby asked, and Eddy shrugged. He felt Luther's head with gentle fingers. ''I don't feel any cracks. I reckon he'll be fine once he comes to.''

''We may not have that long to wait,'' I reminded.

''Well, in that case, we'll just have to hurry him along,'' Bobby said. He stood and made a move to the bar, stopping as his eyes fell on Chub's body. He looked at me with a question in his eyes. ''Chub?''

''Yeah, he tried to take on Riley Hunt,'' I answered.

Bobby took off his hat and shook his head sadly. ''Chub was a good man. He wasn't really cut out for this, but he always wanted to be a part of the crowd. He shoulda known better than to tangle with Riley.''

''He more than likely saved our bacon,'' I said.

Bobby nodded absently. "Poor Chub, he always wanted to be a known man. I guess he ain't gonna make it now." Bobby stared at the body for a long second, then abruptly spun on his heel and stalked behind the bar. He took a mug from beneath the bar and drew a beer from the keg. He tasted the beer, then vaulted lightly over the bar. He started to pour the beer on Luther, but Eddy stopped him.

"Do you think that is a good idea? The shock of that might not be good for him."

Bobby smiled, shrugging his shoulders. "He's tough. Besides, he's lollygagged long enough." He started to pour, then glanced at Eddy again. "Anyway, if they trap us in here, that ain't gonna be good for any of us."

As the beer splashed against his face, Luther sputtered and groaned, his eyes fluttering open. "Bobby," he whispered hoarsely. "I shoulda know if there was trouble, you'd be right in the middle of it." He touched a finger to his face, then put the finger in his mouth. "Beer. That'll be going on your bill."

"What!" Bobby screeched. "I used that to wake you up."

Luther groaned and struggled to set up. "If I know you, you helped yourself to a drink or two before you woke me."

"You two can settle your money differences later. Let's get out of here," I suggested.

"Good idea," Bobby agreed as he and Eddy boosted Luther to his feet. "Can you walk?"

Luther put one hand out to steady himself and rubbed the back of his head with the other. His face was white as milk and he swayed like a sapling in a high wind, but he nodded grimly. "I can travel."

"You know of a way out of this place?" I asked, keeping an eye outside. The battle seemed to be slacking off. Now was the time to leave.

"Oh, yeah," Bobby assured me with a grin. "I don't think anyone else knows of it. Riley will go crazy wondering where you went."

"You lead off. I'll cover the rear," I instructed.

"You sure you're up to it?" Bobby asked doubtfully. "That leg looks a mite stiff."

"You know the way. You lead off. Don't worry about me, I'll be right behind you."

"You're the boss," Bobby said. He opened the back door, looked out, then ducked outside. Eddy and Luther followed quickly. I took a last respectful look at Chub's body. I felt like there was something I should say or do, but I couldn't think of anything. I tipped my hat to him, then scrambled after the others.

Twenty yards ahead of me and wearing a daring grin, Bobby led the way, weaving between the buildings. With Eddy and Luther right behind him, he rounded the corner of the bunkhouse.

I hurried to follow them but wasn't getting along very good. My bum hurt like the devil every time I took a step. 'Course, on my best day, I ain't no gazelle, but I was sure trying. Then I ran right into Jim as the outlaw rushed out of the bunkhouse. He had an armload of shells that fell to the ground as we crashed together.

Stumbling back, Jim's eyes widened as he recognized me. He grabbed his pistol from the holster, firing quickly. He fired too quickly, his bullet going wide.

I took my time, squeezing off a shot. The bullet drilled him in the chest, driving him to the ground. I didn't take the time to see if he was dead. To tell the truth, I didn't want to know. Dead men, even skunks like Jim, don't rest easy on a man's conscience.

Breaking into a hitching run, I staggered around the corner of the bunkhouse, then stopped dead in my tracks. For a second, I held my hurt leg and stared, a feeling of dread smacking me head on. There was nothing behind the bunkhouse except a rock wall towering into the sky a hundred feet. My friends had disappeared!

A panic rising from the pit of my stomach, I looked both ways. Where could they have gone? I didn't get long to ponder the question.

I heard a shout and the sound of running feet. For a second, I ran in circles, unsure of which way to jump. I decided the barn offered the best protection. The bunkhouse was closer, but I didn't want to take the chance of it being occupied.

I scooted for the barn, ducking low as I crossed the open space between the buildings. Somebody shot at me, but I didn't slow to see who it was.

I was running flat out, when I burst through the door of the barn. I'd been scared and hadn't even thought about my leg. The minute I remembered it, the danged thing buckled on me. I managed one more step, then crashed headfirst into a stall. My weight wiped the gate smooth out, smashing it into toothpicks.

I fell facefirst in the straw, my head buzzing and my left arm and shoulder numb. The horse in the stall began to dance and paw as he fought the tether rope. He stepped on my back, nearly driving the wind from me. Covering my head with my hands, I rolled to the edge of the stall. I took a second to catch my breath, then picked up my pistol from where it had fallen. I brushed the straw from the weapon and touched my extra pistol to make sure it was still behind my belt.

My hands climbing the partition between the stalls, I pulled myself to my feet. That fool horse promptly stepped sideways, squashing me against the partition.

While I tried to push the horse away from me, a man rushed through the barn door, his eyes darting about as he tried to spot me. I rested my six-gun across the horse's back, firing just as he spied me.

I hit him, all right, but not solid. He dropped his gun and scurried outside. I snapped another shot at him, which missed. I heard a sound behind me. A man had his face pressed against the yellowed window. I shot at him twice, but that fool horse bumped me, spoiling my aim. I broke the window and put the fear into the man, but I didn't hurt him any. I swore at myself. I was trapped and outnumbered. I couldn't afford any more misses.

A chunky man in a red shirt darted across the wide doorway in front of me. I tracked him with the pistol for just a second, then squeezed the trigger. The gun only clicked. It was empty!

Riley Hunt walked calmly into the barn, his pistol trained on my head. "You're out of bullets and out of luck," he said.

Chapter Fifteen

"Throw that gun down,'' Hunt ordered. I tossed it away, my spirits sinking as two men rushed into the barn, taking positions beside Hunt. One of them had wild, bulging eyes, the other was a fat, greasy man. Both of them smiled at Hunt.

''Come out from there,'' Hunt ordered. With little choice, I pushed the horse away from me and edged out of the stall. The extra gun I'd taken from Chub was still behind my belt; I could feel it gouging me in the belly, but I couldn't draw it. Not with that horse wedged up against me.

''Hey, boss, where's that good-looking filly he came in with?'' the fat man asked, rubbing his hands together. He smiled, revealing broken teeth.

"Where is she?" Hunt demanded. All three of them glanced around the barn for Eddy.

I grabbed that pistol from my belt and dropped to the ground. I fired as I hit the ground. My first bullet hit Hunt in the hip, spinning him around and knocking him flat. Shifting my aim, I shot at the fat man. My two bullets smashed Fatty back and flattened him against the wall. He stood on his toes, his pistol dribbling from his fingers, then he pitched facefirst into the hard packed-dirt floor.

All of a sudden, in the absence of gunfire, the barn seemed as quiet as a church on Monday night. By now, Hunt had wormed into a stall. Somehow I'd lost track of the bug-eyed man. I didn't know if he ducked outside or took cover and was hiding somewhere in the barn. Right then, I decided, I didn't care. I was bruised and sore from the tip of my hat to the point of my boots. And I was mad. I'd had enough of being shoved around.

I flipped open the cylinder of my pistol. Three shots left. Three shots weren't nowhere near enough to fight my way out of here, but it was a plenty to put an end to Riley Hunt.

In the saloon, I'd seen what kind of sick, twisted man Hunt was. If ever there was a man that needed to be scotched, it was Riley Hunt. Snapping the cylinder shut, I set my jaw firm. I was going to be the man to finish the job.

Grinding my teeth, I pushed up to my feet. Ol' bug-eye broke from behind a stack of feed. Pivoting on the balls of my feet, I snapped two shots at him. The first burned his neck and the second smashed his shoulder and sent him rolling head over heels.

I felt the bullet whiz past me, but I didn't dive for cover, though. I was way too mad for that.

I whipped my pistol around, firing across my body. I hit Hunt in the arm, the slug knocking the gun from Hunt's fist. For a second, a wave of desperation crashed over me. I was plumb out of bullets and I hadn't polished off Riley Hunt. I hadn't even knocked the fight out of him. Even as I stared at him, he bent over, trying to pick up his fallen pistol with his left hand.

I threw my empty pistol at him, then followed it in a long dive. I slammed into Hunt as he tried to swing the pistol into firing position. I slammed him back, but I didn't knock the gun from his fist. Nor did I get my arms wrapped around him. He bounced away from me and smacked against the wall.

As he steadied himself against the wall, I decided I wasn't as tough as I first thought. All of a sudden, I didn't want to take on that pistol with my bare hands. I flopped over the dividing partition and into the next stall. I heard the crash of Riley's gun, but had no idea where the bullet hit. It didn't bump into me and that was all I was really worried about.

In the next stall, I looked around frantically for something . . . anything to use for a weapon. There were a couple of saddles hanging on the fence; I glanced at them hoping there might be a rifle in one of the saddle boots, but I don't have that kind of luck.

All I could find was a bucket. Now, a bucket ain't much of a weapon to use against a six-shooter. 'Course, I wasn't exactly in any position to be choosy. Glad to have it, I latched onto that bucket with both hands.

My breath coming in great, ragged gasps, I clutched the handle of that bucket and waited. I saw the top of Riley's head first, then his face came into view as he stepped up to the divider between the stalls.

I reckon, if he woulda just fired, he would likely have salted me away. He didn't, though. He was in a talking mood and wanted to gloat a little. I didn't know what he was going to say, but I didn't want to hear it. When he stopped and opened his mouth, I swung that bucket as hard as I could. I aimed to clobber him over the head, but he musta seen it comin', cause he jerked his head back. That bucket smacked him across the forearm, knocking the gun from his fist.

Before I had a chance to scoop up the weapon, Riley dove over the partition. He plowed into me with his shoulder and knocked me for a loop. As he stooped to retrieve his pistol, I lunged out of the stall. I slammed the stall gate behind me and was looking for a place to hide when I heard a tremendous crash. I looked back to see Riley run headfirst into the stall gate, his head ramming plumb through the wooden gate. His tongue hung out of his mouth and he wasn't moving. Now, I didn't know if he was dead or not, and to tell the truth, I really didn't care. All I cared about was getting out of this barn with all my parts and pieces. I lurched to my feet and staggered out of the stall. I stood in the center of the barn, wondering what I was going to do now. Slowly the sound of gunfire sunk into my brain. I cocked my eyes, listening to the battle raging outside. I didn't have the foggiest idea what was going on out there, but it sounded like one humdinger of a battle.

I was still trying to get my breath when a man in a faded blue shirt rushed into the barn. He didn't see me since he was looking back behind him and firing as he looked. Taking into consideration that he had a gun in his fist and I didn't, I decided I best do something before he got around to noticing me.

I grabbed him around the head and took him down like you'd bulldog a steer. Once I got him on the ground, I held his head in my armpit and walloped him until he quit thrashing and struggling.

I'd had enough. I made up my mind, I was getting out of this miserable hole in the ground right now. I picked up Riley Hunt's gun and loaded it with shells from his belt. I appropriated another pistol and loaded it as well. Sticking both guns in my belt, I looked at the horses in the barn. Finally, I picked a big gray horse with black spots on his hindquarters.

I backed the gray horse out of a stall and slipped a bridle on him. I didn't bother with a saddle, I just crawled on bareback.

That gray horse was big and powerful and when I booted him in the ribs, he jumped out of that barn like he'd been shot out of a cannon. Holding the reins in my teeth and guiding the horse with my knees, I drew both of my pistols.

As we pounded out of the barn, a man snapped a shot at me with a rifle. I felt the bullet hit me and it felt like I'd been kicked by a mule. I almost lost my seat and had to throw my arm around the horse's neck to stay aboard. To tell the truth, I was ready to stop and give up, but that gray horse had other ideas. He pointed his ears at the man that shot me and took after him like a crazed bull.

Me and that horse bore down on him as he tried to work the lever of his rifle for another shot. We were right on top of him so instead of wasting a shot, I slashed at his head with one of my pistols. He saw the blow coming and bobbed his head, but the barrel of that gun still smacked him on the top of the shoulder, knocking him clear of us.

I pointed that gray horse for the cut between the rock walls. A group of men were still guarding the entrance. They whirled to face me, surprise written on their faces.

I didn't give them a chance to recover. I drew down on them with my pistols, blazing away with both hands. I don't know if I hit any of them or not. I wasn't really aiming; I just threw lead in their direction as fast as I could pull the triggers. Judging from the way they scattered, I don't reckon I did hit any of them, but I sure scared them.

One danged fool up and decided to hold his ground. We were right on top of him, so I drew back my foot and booted him right square in the chest. The force of that kick sent him rolling, but it also wiped me clean off the back of that gray horse.

I hit flat on my shoulders, the breath completely driven from my lungs. I lay flat on my back, knowing I was beaten. I could hear shooting and running all around me, but I couldn't do anything about it. Them outlaws could come and finish me off. I didn't care.

Chapter Sixteen

I don't know how long I lay there, but when someone leaned over me, it wasn't one of the outlaws. It was Weeb. He stared down at me, then spit and shook his head. "Boy, you must think you are ten men, the way you took off after them boys. I gotta admit, you're a fighter, though. You sure put a dent in them."

"How did you get here?" I asked, feeling woozy as a fly at the bottom of a beer mug.

Weeb laughed and slapped his knee. "You let us in. We was at the head of the canyon, keeping them fellers busy while you slipped out the back." He stopped and scratched his jaw with the barrel of his pistol. "How come you didn't slip out the back? Well, shoot, I reckon that don't matter now. Anyway, when you scattered them boys we came hotfooting it up the notch. Bobby and Luther were behind the stable and we caught them fellers in a crossfire. They lost their stomachs for that real quick. You should see it, we got a mess of them tied up in the saloon.''

``What about Hunt?'' I asked. ``Is he dead?''

``Naw, we got him trussed up in the barn.'' Weeb chuckled and shook his head. ``I don't reckon he's feeling too spiffy, though. He lost a lot of hide when we pulled his head out of that gate. 'Course, I don't reckon that will bother him. Not where he's going.''

``Where's Eddy?'' I asked, hoping I'd heard the last of Riley Hunt.

``She's a-comin','' Weeb answered. ``We wanted to make sure we had all them outlaws rounded up first.''

It wasn't long before she and Bobby came running up. ``Are you all right?'' Eddy asked breathlessly. To tell the truth, I wasn't right sure. ``You been shot!'' she exclaimed, then branded Weeb with a scorching stare. ``How come you didn't attend to his wounds?''

Weeb cocked his head and rubbed the gray stubble on his cheeks. ``We was visiting,'' he said, like that ought to explain everything.

``What happened?'' Bobby asked as Eddy tore open my shirt. ``You was supposed to follow us out the back way,'' he said.

``I ran into Jim. By the time I settled with him, you guys were gone. I looked for your back door, but I couldn't find it.''

Bobby laughed grimly. "Yeah, it ain't easy to find if you don't know where it's at." Bobby admitted. "We got to the top and waited. After you didn't show up, me and Luther snuck back down to see what happened."

Luther chuckled. "I don't know what happened in that barn. All I know is, we kept chasing fellers in there and they didn't come back out."

"Boy, you can say that again," Weeb roared. "For a big, slowlooking lug, you sure are a scraper. We found guys lying everywhere in that barn, and it will be a long time 'fore any of them feel up to dancing." He stopped and licked his lips. "When we get you back to Miles City, we're gonna throw you the biggest party you ever did see."

I guess the mention of that party put them folks into a traveling mood, 'cause they loaded me up on a horse and hauled me to town, when, truthfully, I would have enjoyed resting a bit more. Still, the trip didn't kill me, so I reckon I should be grateful.

They had their party, but of course, I didn't get to go. No, sir, I was stuck in the hotel with that crabby old doc prodding me. "Who bandaged this wound?" the doc asked as he finished up.

"I did," Eddy said, cringing back a little.

"Not bad," he said and grunted. "A little tighter would have been better," he said, gathering his stuff. He glared down at me over the top of his glasses. "You get some rest."

After the doc left, Luther stepped up holding his hat in his hand. "For some reason, I feel like I should thank you," he said.

"I reckon it's the other way around. We owe you our lives. When you get out of jail, come look us up. There's a job waiting for you," I offered.

Luther smiled and put his hat on. "I'm not going to jail. They couldn't find any Wanted posters on me, so Sheriff Len turned me loose." Luther paused, taking his hat back off. "As for the job, I might come looking one day, but first I got some things I have to set right first."

"Take care of yourself, Luther," I said, shaking his hand.

As he left, Eddy sat down on the bed, taking my hand in hers. "Does it hurt much?" she asked.

I wanted to shrug it off, but that did hurt, so I just shook my head. "I guess we'll have to put off buying the cattle till next year," I said.

"That's the plan. We decided to head back home as soon as you're able to travel," Eddy told me.

"Soon as we get home, I'm going to start building our house, so we can be married." Eddy didn't say anything, she just held my hand tighter. "I reckon, once the house is done, if you wanted to have them kids over for a week or so, I could stand it," I finally managed to say, but it wasn't easy.

"They're waiting outside. They want to see you."

I really didn't want to see them. I figured I had suffered enough, but I reckoned if Riley Hunt couldn't kill me, I could survive one more meeting with them kids. They came in and I hardly recognized them. They looked like they had been licked by a cow they were so slicked up.

I looked up at Joan, and she looked every inch a pretty young lady. "Are you going to be all right staying with Bertha and Tom?"

She smiled down at me, a hint of mischief in her eyes.

"Sure, we know how to get by."

I closed my eyes and thanked the good Lord that I wasn't Preacher Tom. That man was going to have his hands full.